"Are you saying you want to be friends while you're working at the company?"

Friends?

Was that really what she thought he wanted? He was so aware of her—her scent, the way her skin softened under his fingers—that he could *feel* her and they weren't even touching. He clenched his fingers into a fist to keep from reaching out to her. "I'm not sure anything platonic would work for us. But we didn't take time to become friends before."

"Then you're saying friends with benefits—because of our off-the-charts sex life?"

"Is that such a bad thing?"

He caught her gaze then. The electricity no longer just hummed in the boathouse lights. Instead, sparks danced between them, caught in the way neither of them could seem to look away. He saw conflicted feelings in her dark brown eyes. But also saw the longing.

He just needed to be patient.

* * *

The Twin Birthright is part of the Alaskan Oil Barons series, the eight-book saga from *USA TODAY* bestselling author Catherine Mann!

Dear Reader,

Thank you for checking out my Alaskan Oil Barons series! I welcome the chance to reach out to you with these letters. I believe the reader community is like a sprawling, extended family. I come from a large, loving family and appreciate the joy and support that comes with that extended connection. Maybe that's why I enjoy writing family sagas so much—like the Steeles and Mikkelsons in this series.

With *The Twin Birthright*, the Steele family is expanding yet again, bigger than ever with the addition of twins for Naomi and her former fiancé Royce. Yes, Naomi and Royce from *The Double Deal* and *The Baby Claim* are back in the spotlight!

Will they get it right this time and nab their happily-ever-after? Read on to see!

I love to hear from my reader community family, so please do feel free to reach out to contact me via my website, www.catherinemann.com.

Happy reading!

Cheers,

Cathy

Catherine Mann

www.CatherineMann.com

CATHERINE MANN

THE TWIN BIRTHRIGHT

ISBN-13: 978-1-335-97149-4

The Twin Birthright

This edition published by arrangement with Harlequin Books S.A.

For questions and comments about the quality of this book, please contact us at CustomerService@Harlequin.com.

Printed in U.S.A.

USA TODAY bestselling author **Catherine Mann** has won numerous awards for her novels, including both a prestigious RITA® Award and an *RT Book Reviews* Reviewers' Choice Award. After years of moving around the country bringing up four children, Catherine has settled in her home state of South Carolina, where she's active in animal rescue. For more information, visit her website, catherinemann.com.

Books by Catherine Mann

Harlequin Desire

Diamonds in the Rough

One Good Cowboy
Pursued by the Rich Rancher
Pregnant by the Cowboy CEO

Alaskan Oil Barons

The Baby Claim
The Double Deal
The Love Child
The Twin Birthright

Visit her Author Profile page at Harlequin.com, or catherinemann.com, for more titles.

"A daughter may outgrow your lap,
but she will never outgrow your heart."
—Anonymous

To my daughters, Haley and Maggie.
It's been a joy and honor having watched
you both grow into miraculous women.
I love you!

One

Some women dreamed of giving birth in a hospital, husband holding her hand.

Some visualized delivering at home, man of her dreams breathing alongside.

No one fantasized about bringing a new life into the world in an SUV, in a snowstorm, with her ex-fiancé playing "catch the baby." Or in Naomi Steele's case, *babies. Plural.* Two of them. The first of which was due to make an appearance with the next…

"Push! Push, Naomi, push," Royce Miller's soft, deep voice radiated confidence in the confines of his Suburban, heater blasting inside, snow pelting the vehicle outside.

"I am pushing, damn it. I've been pushing." Because there wasn't any need to wait. No help was on the way. Cell phone reception was almost nil on a deserted highway north of Anchorage, Alaska. Sporadic bursts of connectivity offered only minimal reassurance that anyone had heard their pleas for rescue when she'd gone into labor a month early.

Even if help could make it to them through this Alaska blizzard.

The seats of the SUV had been flattened, blankets under her, an emergency kit including first aid spread out beside her. Thank goodness he'd kept his vehicle well stocked in the event of being stranded in a storm. But then of course he had. He was always analytical, organized, the brilliant scientist and professor who planned for any—and every—contingency.

She had her own analytical side as an attorney, but was more known for her flair for the dramatic, which had served her well in the courtroom more than once.

Royce knelt on the floor, his muscular body wedged in, but he still managed to look comfortable. At ease. In control.

Pain ripped through her, her whole body locked in one big muscle spasm beyond anything she'd read about or heard about in child birthing classes. She understood intellectually that a couple of pushes wouldn't get the job done, especially for a first-time mom, but she was so done. Ready to quit. Close to tears and burning to scream, but she didn't want to put any additional burden on Royce when he had to be afraid, in spite of his calm demeanor.

Beads of sweat rolled down his face.

And she knew she wasn't going to get any relief with this contraction. Disappointment stung even as the pain eased. She exhaled and sagged back. Taking the moment to store up every kernel of energy as best she could.

Light from outside grew dimmer with the ending day and thick storm. Their car lights provided minimal illumination. Royce had hung two flashlights with bungie cords. She didn't want to think about what would happen if this took too long and they ran out of gasoline.

After months on bed rest for her blood pressure, Naomi had been released by the doctor *today.* Once they'd finished the appointment, all she'd wanted was a simple afternoon drive and to celebrate a less restricted final month of her pregnancy. She was sure about their due date, since hers had been an in vitro fertilization, with a donor sperm. When she'd made the decision, she'd been worried her chance to be a mother was passing her by; that was before she met eccentric research scientist Royce Miller. Their relationship had been doomed from the start. She'd been just over two months pregnant and it had been too easy for him to use her babies as a substitute for his unresolved past.

Royce patted her knee with his broad hand. "Are you warm enough?" The wind howled, nearly drowning out his words. "I've got my coat ready for the babies, but I can give you my shirt."

She knew those beads of sweat on his forehead had nothing to do with the temperature in the vehicle.

"I'm fine, really." Even if she had been cold—which she wasn't because currently her body was on fire with pain—she couldn't take anything more from Royce. He'd given up so much of his life for her, even after they'd ended their engagement. He'd seemed to feel obligated to stay by her side until the babies were born. Every day since the breakup had been bittersweet torture. Being with him filled her with regret, sadness but—ultimately—resolve.

And she'd needed that resolve to stand her ground—she'd made the right decision in ending things—and stand up to this silently stubborn man. He'd steadfastly continued to show up with his own agenda.

Like insisting on driving her to the doctor's office today even though she had over a dozen family members who would have stepped in to help. After the smooth-as-silk OB visit, Royce hadn't driven far and the weather report had been clear as a bell. They'd been doing everything right—

Another contraction hit her hard and fast, with minimal buildup to warn her. She held back the urge to shout, and forced even breaths in and out—well, as even as possible. The distant sound of Royce counting to ten grounded her until, finally, the contraction subsided and she could relax again.

He was always so careful and precise. Unlike her reckless self. They'd broken up twice, and the second time had stuck. Well, stuck in that they stopped sleeping together and any mention of the love they'd once shared was off-limits.

And like karma laughing in her face at supposed boundaries, here she was, stuck in a snowstorm with him, just like the day they'd met nearly six months ago. Theirs had been a whirlwind romance, with an engagement that had ended nearly as quickly as it had begun.

They were just too different. They wanted different things.

At first, they'd struggled with her need to prove her strength and independence, a by-product of her teenage battle with cancer. His overprotective ways had been stifling. But eventually they'd found a balance in that. Even so, in the end, there'd been another, larger problem lurking, one core to their personalities. Something they couldn't change.

He was a brilliant, reclusive man who thrived on his work, but battled emotional insecurity, searching for a "replacement" family. She was an extrovert who flourished in the courtroom and in the company of her big, boisterous family. She'd nearly gone stir-crazy in their secluded cabin. And he'd been climbing the walls when they'd tried living in the city. She couldn't bear to see him lose what made him so special in the first place. They'd had to admit they were just too different.

And he was an admirable man. That ripped at her most of all. Still, she'd tried to push him away, but no matter what she'd said and done, he wouldn't go. His stubbornness only solidified her opinion that any emotion he'd invested in their time together was all about the babies.

He had insisted on staying in touch during her pregnancy, helping, even though the babies weren't his biological children. Seeing him was beyond difficult. Her heart broke over and over again. But given that he consulted for her family's oil business, there was no avoiding each other completely. They had to learn to coexist peacefully.

She just hadn't expected that coexisting to include him parked between her bent knees delivering her twins—

Another pain gripped her, and as hard as she tried to force those breaths in and out, panic built. "I'm scared," she gasped, fighting against the pain, which only made it worse. "What if something's wrong? We're out in the middle of nowhere—"

"Breathe, Naomi, breathe. Everything's going to be okay."

"Like you have—" she huffed a half-hearted breath "—any choice—" another gasp "—but to say that."

"All was well at your last checkup..." He paused, then continued, his voice intense, "I see the baby's head coming closer. You're doing it. Come on, Naomi."

"How do you know?" she groused, while pushing, gripping the door handle.

He rested a hand on her knee, catching her gaze with his deep brown eyes as the contraction subsided. He was steady. In control. "I've actually delivered a baby before."

"Really?" She wanted to believe it. So much.

"I never told you that?" The smile on his handsome face lit hope inside her.

"No, you didn't." But then they hadn't known each other even a year yet. So much passion—and then heartbreak—had been packed into a short time. They hadn't been able to keep their hands off each other from the start. They'd let that sexual connection take precedence over getting to know each other.

"Let's get these babies into the world and I'll tell you all about it."

The next contraction cut short anything she might have thought about saying, if she could even remember words. Pain gripped her. More powerful than any of the others. Pressure built, intensified until she lost track of counting. It surely had to be more than ten—

The pressure released and the vehicle filled with...cries. Her baby. Tears welled in Naomi's eyes, blurring the vision of Royce holding her newborn child up for her to see.

"It's a girl," he said, emotion clogging his voice as he confirmed the gender ultrasounds had shown. But hearing it now still carried such a momentous thrill.

"She's okay?"

"A healthy set of lungs, ten fingers and ten toes."

Once Royce tied off the cord and wrapped the infant in his parka, he passed the bundle to Naomi, who held out her arms. She cradled the precious weight against her, marveling in gazing at her child for the first time. Love swelled in her heart and she looked at Royce. Just as another contraction gripped her. He reached over her to settle the baby at her side.

Naomi gasped, "I guess…now…I know with absolute…certainty that you have…delivered a baby before."

His low chuckle filled the SUV just before the pressure built again, until she felt the familiar release. Followed by another infant cry.

"Naomi, you have another healthy baby girl." Royce's joy was mixed with a hint of a tremble that relayed yes, he must have been more nervous than he let on.

How could he not have been?

But all that mattered now was that her twins were alive. Safe. She sagged back in relief, holding her first child against her side and reaching out her arm for the other.

Royce wrapped the second newborn in her pink parka and passed the baby over. Naomi stared into those wide curious eyes and thought of her sister, Breanna, who'd died over a decade before, along with their mother.

The connection between Naomi and her sister had been strong. They were fraternal twins. Although people had often thought Breanna was Marshall's twin since she favored him so closely when they were young, and they were inseparable. Who knew how her sister would have looked as an adult since she'd died so young. Naomi swallowed back a lump of emotion and focused on the present. This joy.

Royce settled her legs and rested a blanket over her, before stretching up to lie beside her. "I've sent out texts for help. Let's just enjoy the babies and stay warm while we wait."

He climbed onto the reclined seats, curving his muscular body against her, somehow making room for himself in spite of the seat belts draped overhead and flashlights suspended from bungees. He was so familiar, and Lord, how she'd missed the feel of him, this closeness. She'd once dreamed of them like this, except spooned together in a hospital bed with the babies, all of them a family.

She looked over at him and found him studying the babies, which allowed her to stare at him longer. He was so much more than broodingly handsome good looks. The appeal was more than his leanly muscle-bound body on display in his chest-hugging T-shirt. And yeah, he got bonus points for the thick dark hair a hint too long, as if he'd forgotten to get a haircut, tousled like he'd just gotten out of bed.

All enticing. Sure.

But it was always his eyes that held her. Those windows to the soul. To the man. A man with laser-sharp intelligence in his deep brown gaze that pierced straight to the core of her and seemed to say, *Bring it, woman. I can keep up.*

And he had. He'd been willing to make every compromise to secure her—and her babies—in his life in a sad effort to recreate what he'd lost when his former fiancée had miscarried, then walked away.

Naomi couldn't risk hoping for a future with him, now more than ever, with the stability and well-being of these two precious little lives counting on her. If only they could all four stay just like this forever, warm and secure together while the storm raged outside.

A crack echoed, interrupting her thoughts, and she glanced up sharply to see an ice-laden tree fall across the hood of Royce's SUV.

Compartmentalizing was easier said than done.

Royce Miller wanted to be the cool scientist, detached. But this was Naomi. Her babies.

Not his.

His chest ached as if he'd sucked in a gulp of frozen air. He tucked his arm around her tighter as she catnapped, the babies sleeping against her chest.

Earlier, while she'd nursed the babies, he'd sent

out a slew of additional texts, hoping one would make it through the storm. The SUV was still running, and he had extra fuel in the emergency kit. But once they needed that, he would have to try to move the tree off the hood. Hopefully, the SUV would be in shape to drive, although that was a last resort in this weather. Especially with two infants and no car seats.

He'd turned off all but one of the flashlights now to preserve batteries. His heart still slugged against his ribs in the aftermath. He could still barely wrap his brain around the fact that he'd delivered the babies. That Naomi was okay. Relief mixed with the reality that until he had them all in a hospital, he couldn't breathe easy.

After scanning the babies, checking that their chests rose and fell evenly, he glanced at the pulse in Naomi's neck. He grounded himself in the steady rhythm.

"Royce?" she whispered.

Her soft voice drew his gaze to her face. The look in her tired but beautiful eyes was…incredible. Shining brighter than the flashlight overhead.

He'd had her, and she'd slipped away from him.

It still grated deep in his gut how she'd pushed him away, given up on what they'd shared, what they could have had in the future. It was hard as hell to forgive how she'd just let go.

He brushed back her hair from her forehead, the

softness of her skin soaking into him. "Here we are again, stuck together."

"Your SUV is almost as big as that little cabin you were staying in." She smiled at him wryly. "Somehow, we always manage the craziest scenarios. The way you chased that bear off my car when we first met."

Memories of that day filled him. How she'd bluffed her way into his cabin retreat to convince him to sign on his research with her family's oil business—Alaska Oil Barons, Incorporated. He'd been resistant, but man, how she'd won him over with her lawyer skills—and her smile.

And her bravado in the face of an unexpected grizzly climbing on the hood of her vehicle when she'd arrived at his cabin. "I suspect you could have handled that massive Pooh Bear yourself."

"I'll take that as a compliment."

"It was intended as one."

She was a gutsy woman with an indomitable spirit he admired. Pulling his gaze away from her intoxicating whiskey-brown eyes, he looked out the window. The snow had turned to sleet, pinging on the rooftop in the silence between them.

Naomi shifted and settled. "Now you've saved me again. And my girls. Maybe I could have handled that bear, but I couldn't have delivered my own babies."

"Happy to help. And even happier everyone's okay." Relief still burned through his veins. So much could have gone wrong. Still could, if help didn't arrive soon. "As much as it seems we have these somewhat similar crazy turns in our lives, a lot is different."

She chuckled hoarsely. "Like the fact that there's not a chance we'll be having sex this time."

He tapped his temple. "I'm intuitive that way."

Except he hadn't been so intuitive at the start. He'd fallen for the deception that brought her into his life. She'd hidden her identity as a Steele, hoping to get an inside scoop on his research, and ultimately lure him into signing on with her family business. He'd seen only her, wanted her, was determined to have her. And he'd ignored all the warning signs. In fact, he could see now how they'd both used sex to avoid talking about the deeper issues that would later tear them apart.

Resting her head on his shoulder, she sighed. "Thank you, so much. You were amazing and calm. I can't believe everything went okay. They're healthy and alive and I'm still here."

"Yes, you are." He swallowed hard.

"They're beautiful." Her voice rang with awe and love.

"That they are." Like their mama. "Have you settled on names yet?"

"Mary for my mother..." She pressed a kiss to the forehead of her firstborn, still wrapped in his jacket. "And I was thinking Breanna and call her Anna—"

she kissed the clenched fist of her baby wrapped in her pink parka "—in honor of my sister."

Both of whom had died in a plane crash.

He knew well what a mark her sister and mother's deaths had left on her ability to believe happiness could last. Her teenage bout with cancer had piled onto that doubt, chipping away at what remained of her capacity for trust in happy endings.

"That's a lovely tribute. What about middle names?"

"Mary Jaqueline, after both of my parents, Mary and Jack. And I hope you won't mind if I name the other Breanna Royce." Naomi's eyes filled with emotion and a sheen of regret. "You've been here for me, but I understand if—"

"That's perfect. Thank you. I'm honored." Emotion, too much, threatened to steal his focus. He sealed it off and looked for tangible, logical facts. "I would guess they each weigh nearly six pounds. That's remarkable for twins a month early."

She studied him for an intense moment before blinking and glancing away. "No wonder I looked as big as a house."

"You were—and are—beautiful."

She rolled her eyes. "It's nice not to be arguing with a woman who just gave birth in a car."

"I don't fight."

"True." She crinkled her nose, shadows chasing across her face. "But you seethe, holding it in either out of some reclusive habit, or fear of spiking the blood pressure of the pregnant woman." She touched his arm lightly, her nails short and painted a pale pink. "I mean that nicely. You've been kind when you had every right to hate me."

Her words stabbed him clean through. "I could never hate you."

"We're just wrong for each other."

He couldn't deny that, as much as it hurt to admit. Things had moved so fast with them. And then they were done.

"Life's complicated." He studied each baby's face, their features imprinting themselves in his mind. In his heart. "But right now, it feels blessedly simple."

Or at least he wanted it to be. Here in the dimly lit car, the whistle of the wind cutting through the Alaska night. A dream he'd entertained more than once in the past. Before. A whimsical thought that wasn't like him.

She'd insisted he was trying to replace the fiancée who'd walked out on him after miscarrying their child years ago. That he'd been trying to replace that baby, as well. He couldn't deny those losses had hurt like hell. But the breakup with Naomi had been exponentially worse.

Maybe she was right about his need to fill a hole in his life that had never healed after the baby he'd lost. But all he'd known after breaking up with Naomi was that no matter what had happened between them, he needed to usher the twins into the world before he could walk away.

Light sparked behind his eyes. Becoming stronger and stronger until he couldn't blink it away. He frowned, sitting up, looking outside.

Car lights approached, twin beams streaking ahead, an emergency light strobing. Help had arrived. Thank God. Yet with that help came another realization.

As much as he'd thought he could cut ties once the babies were born, he still couldn't walk away. Not tonight.

Two

Naomi shivered under the blankets in the ambulance as she stretched out on the gurney. She had no reason to be cold. The heater was blasting and the emergency technicians had piled blankets on top of her.

Supposedly it was the aftermath of childbirth making her teeth clatter together. That and relief. Her two little girls—Mary and Anna—had been checked over thoroughly and both declared healthy miracles.

Twins, born in a car, in a snowstorm.

Amazing.

Both her babies were bundled up and being secured by the younger of the two techs in preparation for the ride to the hospital. A pediatrician would be waiting for them there.

Her teeth chattered faster and she searched beyond the open back door for Royce. He stood a few feet away, under a spotlight the techs had placed outside. The halogen beam shone down on his hair, made all the darker by the dampness from a fresh sprinkle of snowflakes collecting and melting. She heard the low, confident rumble of his voice. The tones grounded her with reassurance far more than the blankets. Holding strong to keep him at a distance proved hard right now, with her emotions so close to the surface.

"Thank you," he said to the older of the two techs. "I appreciate your coming out on roads as messy as these."

"That's what we're here for." The medic tugged his knit cap more firmly over his head, wind whipping flurries sideways.

"And they're all really okay." Royce's broad shoulders rose and fell with a sigh so heavy she couldn't miss it.

"Mom's blood pressure is a little higher than we would like, but we're monitoring her and we'll be on the road shortly." He nodded. "You handled everything very well, especially considering the circumstances. The babies both have a ten Apgar score."

"That's good to know. When they were born, they both had blue hands, but they came out crying, actively kicking."

"That's excellent. You did a great job in a tough situation. There's really nothing more anyone could have done in those circumstances."

Royce scrubbed the back of his neck, a gesture she recognized as weariness. "Other than not go for an impromptu scenic ride with a pregnant woman."

"You can beat yourself up later, Dad." The older man clapped Royce on the shoulder.

Dad? Naomi's throat closed and she bit her lip against a tremble.

Royce shrugged. "I'm not…their dad."

The pain in his voice tore at her heart. For him, for herself and for her children. She and Royce had made such plans for the future. He was a good man who would have loved her children as much as if they were his own. If only she could have escaped the feeling he was filling a void left by the loss of his own child.

By the loss of his fiancée, a woman he'd known so much longer than his and Naomi's few, intense months together.

Turning, he walked toward the ambulance, stepping up on the bumper and then inside, his eyes trained on Naomi, his broad shoulders nearly filling the opening.

The ambulance shifted again with the arrival of the other tech, angling past him. "My bad, man. I assumed you two were married."

Royce shook his head. "Not married. Not a couple. Not the dad. Just a…friend."

"Then I'm sorry, sir." The man smiled apologetically. "You'll have to step out of the rig. You can follow us in the tow truck."

Royce's face went tight for a moment before he shot her a forced smile. "Naomi, I'll see you and the girls at the hospital. I promise."

He stepped back out and the void where he'd been seemed to expand. Naomi's stomach sank as the doors closed, sealing Royce out. He dropped out of sight.

She thought she'd gotten used to the idea of doing this on her own, but having him with her through the birth of the babies had felt so right, the connection between them fragile, but there.

The door to the rig slammed, and they pulled onto the road, taking with them the last hint of how things might have been.

Royce couldn't will his feet to move, eyes fixed on the glass that separated him from the nurse's station where the twins were being settled. He watched the staff cradle the girls, tugging a tiny T-shirt and cap on each newborn before swaddling them in a blanket. Try as he might, he couldn't avert his gaze now that he'd finally made it to the hospital.

The trek here looped in his mind as he remembered the sinking feeling in his chest, being stuck in a damn tow truck with no rights to Naomi or the babies. He'd called to postpone his guest lecture series at the university. He'd also arranged for a car to pick him up in the morning, and sent an email to his administrative assistant at the oil company to start the paperwork for a replacement SUV. A new version of the one he'd had. He didn't like change in his life. From a make and model of a vehicle to a brand of boots.

At least he hadn't been stuck finding a ride tonight. The driver had taken pity on him and brought him all the way to the hospital before leaving with the demolished SUV.

Monitors beeped, briefly calling his attention away from the smells of disinfectant and stale coffee. Even late at night, the hospital hummed with activity here in the maternity ward. The low din of a family huddled together waiting to hear the news. A couple of grandparents at the window, tapping. A cart rattled by, pulled by a nurse. A mother walked slowly down the hall, pushing a wheeled hospital bassinet.

A rush of cold air pricked the hairs on the back of his neck as he registered the sound of doors opening. Barely enough time to digest the herd of people flooding in. Naomi's family filled the room, rushing toward him and the glass window pane. Concern became a common, identifiable feature on everyone's brow.

So. Many. Brows.

Her sister, Delaney; two of her brothers, Broderick and Aiden. Broderick's wife, Glenna, and a slew of other Steeles and Mikkelsons, whose faces all started to become a blur after a while, there were so many of them.

So many people here to support Naomi and the girls. That was a good thing. He should be fine with leaving. She didn't want him here. She'd pushed him away.

But he wasn't anywhere near okay with turning his back on them. He needed to see her settled in with the girls after the tumultuous delivery. He could provide a buffer between her and her overprotective family. He'd already sent out messages to excuse himself from work for a few days, his research taking a back burner to this.

Delaney—a shier version of Naomi—tugged her dark ponytail tighter, her eyes welling with tears that glistened even brighter than her diamond stud earrings. "Ohmigod, Royce, what happened to my sister?"

"The babies?" Glenna's gaze was direct.

Broderick stepped up behind his wife. "In a snowstorm?"

The Steeles and Mikkelsons were out in full, overwhelming force.

In days past, they would have been at each other's throats. Now they were a unified wall of huge personalities.

Royce shifted toward them, while keeping his body angled enough toward the window that he could still see the infants out of the corner of his eye. "We had just left the doctor's appointment. She got a clean bill of health, so we took a drive to get a bite to eat. The storm came out of nowhere right as she went into labor." He gestured toward the side-by-side warmers, with pediatricians and nurses gathered on the other side of the partition glass. "Those are your nieces."

Delaney stepped closer with a soft, "Oh, my."

Glenna pulled her cell phone from its monogrammed leather case, smiling, her CFO, no-nonsense demeanor fading. "We need photos. Lots. Mom and Jack are already texting me like crazy for updates."

The Steele patriarch and Mikkelson matriarch were on a belated honeymoon.

Broderick, the oldest of the Steele siblings—and a numbers person like his wife—gripped his Stetson. "Well, you certainly came through. I can't thank you enough."

Glenna stepped nearer to her husband, her phone in her hand and her eyes still fixed on the window. "It had to be scary for you."

Teenager Aiden Steele didn't even look up from the screen of his social media feed when he snorted, then said, "Like any guy's going to admit that."

Royce exhaled hard, muttering, "It was scary. As hell."

Broderick's stern face went taut. "Damn straight, it was." He pinned his youngest brother with a quick stare. "Only young fools don't know when to be afraid." He looked back. "Being scared and pushing ahead, that's bravery."

Royce cleared his throat. "I'm just glad everyone's all right," he repeated, for what felt like the millionth time, but knew it could never be said enough to ease the chill inside him. The room started to close in on him with all these people.

Glenna wrapped her arms around herself, visibly trying to calm down as she rubbed her hands over the elbows of a cashmere cardigan. "Marshall—" the middle Steele son "—flew out to get Mom and Jack and bring them back here."

"I'm sure Naomi wouldn't want to interrupt their honeymoon." Royce waved a hand. Despite the difficulties between them, he knew Naomi could do without the fanfare. She wanted to prove she was capable all on her own. And the last thing he wanted was for her stress level to rise right now and have her blood pressure spike as a result.

Jack and Jeannie had certainly waited long enough for a real honeymoon. They'd had to delay their wedding and their trip after Jack's spinal injury in a horseback riding accident. Luckily, he'd made a miraculous recovery after the surgery. They'd gotten married shortly after he'd gotten the neck brace off, but their celebration trip had been further delayed.

Broderick shook his head. "Like Dad was going to take our word for it that his little girl's okay?"

"Fair enough." Royce scrubbed a hand over his bleary eyes. The magnitude of the night's events threatened to overwhelm him until he rocked back a step. "I'm going to find the coffee machine. Text me if you hear any news."

He wouldn't have been able to sit idly by, twiddling his thumbs, until he'd seen Naomi and the babies. He still needed to clamp eyes on them again.

Then he could walk away.

Naomi's shakes had waned, but reality was just as rattling now that she was tucked in her hospital bed.

The magnitude of all that could have gone wrong kept pounding through her head. She'd faced the possibility of death as a teenager with cancer, bringing memories too close to the surface anytime she visited a hospital. But the thought of something happening to her babies?

That scared her more than anything she'd ever experienced.

Hospital beds, even in the maternity ward, never did Naomi's back any favors. The hospital decor spoke of an attempt at making the place seem more like a homey living room, but fell short of the mark. Doing her best to adjust her position, she sat straighter, determined to make a rapid recovery. The interminable bed rest of her pregnancy had made her stir-crazy. She blinked against the harsh lights of the room as her doctor and the pediatrician exited into the too white hallway.

Despite the roadside delivery, the pediatrician had given her a positive report that ought to have put her mind at ease. Instead, Naomi fidgeted, rubbing her fingers together as the redheaded nurse with freckled constellations on her cheeks adjusted the covers and set a glass of room-temperature water on the rolling bedside table.

The nurse closed the door behind her as she left, and the hushed sounds of hallway conversation dimmed.

But Naomi's heart was with her babies. She felt like the exams had taken longer than if she'd delivered the babies here. In fact, her daughters would have to stay in the nursery for observation tonight, since they'd been born in such unusual, unmonitored circumstances. The doctor had told her that once her blood pressure came down, she could see them.

The wait was driving her crazy. At least she didn't have a headache like she'd experienced during pregnancy with her preeclampsia.

Scanning the room, she steadied her gaze on the clock, watching the second hand move like molasses.

The creaking of the door cut through her thoughts, and for a sliver of a second, her heart screamed out for Royce. His calming presence.

Instead of the enigmatic man, Delaney lingered in the doorway, her hand balled into a tense fist as she held on to the sleeves of her green sweater.

Naomi didn't want to think about feeling disappointed.

Had he left? She swallowed hard and focused on her sister with a smile. Extending her arms for a hug, she drew Delaney close, breathing through the physical and emotional pain that racked her body.

"Naomi, the babies are beautiful. Glenna took a million photos already and I'm sure we'll take a million more. How are you?"

"Relieved. Eager to see my children. Grateful Royce was there to help."

"I can't believe you actually delivered in a car." Delaney tugged a chair close to the bedside and sat. "You always did have to one-up me. Two babies and now giving birth in a snowstorm. I'll never top that."

"What can I say?" Naomi shrugged, adjusting her hospital gown. "I strive to overachieve."

"I'm just glad you're all three okay. And the girls, wow. I can't wait to spoil them and buy tons of little pink outfits. I can't believe how tiny they are. So precious. You're so brave."

"I didn't have a choice." Her mind flashed to the terror she'd felt when she realized she wouldn't make it to the hospital. "They were coming out."

"I mean, to be a single mom."

Single.

Not engaged. Not married.

No future with Royce.

She didn't even have her mother to turn to for advice. Naomi fought back tears, working to remind herself of all she had to be grateful for tonight. "It's not like I don't have a ton of support, an even larger family now that Dad's remarried."

But no Royce. No father for her children. It had

all seemed clear when she'd opted for in vitro fertilization with eggs she'd frozen prior to her treatment for cancer. Now everything was…complicated.

In the wake of her relationship with Royce, she better understood all that was missing in her life.

All that might have been for her girls.

"We're here for you." Delaney covered Naomi's hand with hers, careful of the IV. "What's the deal with Royce and you being out there together?"

Naomi sighed. "I should just put a sign on the door explaining, so I don't have to repeat myself. He's been helpful during the pregnancy. He cares about the babies."

"And about you. Be honest." She touched Naomi's forehead, pushing away loose strands of dark hair.

Naomi bit her lip and weighed her sister's words. "We'll always care for each other. But it was just… infatuation. Lust."

"Lust. Whoa. Friendship and lust and caring. Sounds pretty cool to me." She gave an exaggerated wink.

"Trust me," Naomi chuckled softly, "lust is the last thing on my mind right now."

"Understandable. You must be exhausted and I should let you rest." Delaney kissed her forehead. "Is there anything I can get for you? Some water? A nurse?"

"Perhaps ask the nurse to take my blood pressure again to see if I can get up?"

"Absolutely. I'll ask on my way out." She nodded

to the nurse backing through the door. "You're in good hands. I'll see you in the morning."

The middle-aged nurse with silver strands in her jet-black hair barely made it five steps into the room before Naomi's question burst from her lips. "So, do we get to check my blood pressure again?"

Bowed lips drew into a smile, and for a flash of a moment, Naomi saw a glimpse of her mother in the woman. A painful thought, an ache that never seemed to ease.

"Of course, dear. Let's see what your number is now."

Naomi took a deep, steadying breath as the nurse set up the blood pressure machine. *Low. Low. Low.* The wish looped in her mind like a mantra. Her body needed to respond to the command.

An eternity seemed to pass as she stared at the nurse's equipment, waiting for the verdict.

"Well, there, Miss Naomi, I have some good news for you. Your blood pressure is back to normal."

"I'm going to see my babies." Flinging back the sheets, Naomi prepared to swing her legs off the bed.

A gentle hand met her wrist. "Hold on there, dear. I know your pressure's back down, but doctor's orders—you get a wheelchair until he says otherwise."

"As long as I see my children." Naomi took a deep breath, the kind she reserved for stepping into a trial, the type that filled her lungs and soul with determination, then she eased her feet to the floor. She was a little wobbly, but overall better than she expected.

"This is my favorite part of my job, dear."

Naomi craned her head back to examine the nurse. Faint smile lines adorned her cheeks, and the nurse's green eyes were alight.

"Wheeling people around?" Naomi asked, wringing her hands in anticipation. Doctors and nurses rushed past them, carrying charts and chatting hurriedly.

"No. Uniting mother and child. There is nothing as rewarding."

Her pulse pounding like she'd ran a marathon, Naomi swallowed, a lump of nervous anticipation welling in her throat, rendering her unable to speak. As they turned the corner to the nursery, her heart did a cartwheel. Royce. He stood near the babies, decked out in borrowed green scrubs. Looking handsome as ever, as he spoke to the pediatric nurse in a tone so hushed and gentle Naomi couldn't make out a single word he said.

He hadn't left, after all.

Even though she knew he was here for the babies, she still couldn't deny how glad she was to see him. He was a part of her past, but he'd also been a part of this miracle.

She couldn't help but wonder if she was feeling too drawn to him, weakening in an emotional moment. If anything, the other nurse's presence, with reminders of Naomi's mother, made her think of how she should be turning to the relatives she still had. She shouldn't rely on Royce. She wanted to be independent. Even leaning on family would need to be short term—just until she recovered physically—or they could all fall back into the overprotective ways she'd found so stifling as a teen with cancer. She walked a fine line with them in making sure her girls had the joy of the love of a big family.

She smiled her thanks at the nurse who'd helped her down the hall, then rolled the wheelchair toward Royce. "Where is the rest of my family?"

He looked up, lifted an eyebrow and smiled. "Hey, Mama. Good to see you up and about."

The pediatric nurse at the bassinets grinned before turning away and busying herself with another newborn.

Naomi gestured to her wheelchair. "If you can call riding in this 'up.'"

He knelt in front of her. "Your blood pressure's down?"

"Yes. And now I want to see my babies."

"Of course." He reached for the first bundle, Mary, and settled her in the crook of Naomi's arm. Then followed with Anna.

Naomi soaked in the sight of them, clean and sleeping. And beautiful.

She looked up at Royce, finding his eyes locked on hers. She resisted the urge to fidget nervously and reminded herself of who she should be depending on now. "Where's my family? Delaney said they were all here."

She'd especially wanted to see Isabeau who was expecting a baby with Trystan Mikkelson.

"They fawned over your babies and then headed home to give you rest."

"Oh, they just left?" She frowned. That wasn't like them.

"Your blood pressure was up. I sent them away."

She sat up straighter, stunned…irritated. "You did what?"

"It's late. I told them we've got this covered. And they said they'll be back in the morning."

She looked around at the busy staff and kept her voice low. "What gives you the right to decide who stays with me at the hospital?"

"There's another weather warning out, so they left to get ahead of the storm," he said, with such practical calm it set her teeth on edge.

But then she'd always been far quicker to lose her temper than he was.

"And if they'd wanted to stay?"

He stared back at her silently.

Reason trickled through her anger. Nothing could have made her family leave if they hadn't wanted to—or unless they had an ulterior motive. "They're all hoping we'll get back together."

"Maybe. Regardless, I want to help. Is that so bad?"

"I have help. Or rather, I did until you gave them

all their marching orders." She tamped down her anger. "Who's watching your dog?"

His Saint Bernard, Tessie—named in honor of the scientist Tesla—was his big, lovable, constant companion.

"My neighbor's got her. She fine. Don't worry. Just rest."

Sagging back, Naomi relented. She had been surprised at how much it hurt saying goodbye to Tessie when she'd packed up her things at Royce's place. She'd cried more than a few tears into the soft fur.

So many tears. So much grief. She was weary with the hurt.

But it was for the best, because she couldn't risk falling into a relationship with him again.

Naomi cradled her babies, upset, but not wanting to let anything spoil this first night with her girls. And Royce really had been there for her today. They had meant so much to each other once, even if for only a brief time. "I guess this was our plan, back before."

"That it was. I spent a large part of your pregnancy expecting to be their father. It's not so easy for me to just shut that off."

Tears became heavy in her eyes, compromising her vision, as all the words she knew seemed wrong, inadequate. "I'm so sorry for any pain I caused you. I should have known sooner that—"

"Stop. This isn't the time to rehash that." He slid

an arm around her, the strength and heat of him so familiar.

So missed.

She shrugged off his arm and the temptation it held for her to slide into their prior routine. "No offense. But touch me and I'll cry. It's the hormones. And I wish they were in my room with me and everything was...normal."

"Understandable. How about we sit together, you put your feet up here—" he pushed a chair in front of her and lifted her legs to rest on it "—and we'll hold the babies all night long."

She looked up from her daughters into his deep brown eyes, finding his gaze full of emotion, of memories. *Their* memories. And this time there would be no escaping them or hiding from each other. Not now.

As they spent the night together, pretending to be the family they never could be.

Milla Jones pushed the flower cart down the quiet hospital corridor, careful not to wake the sleeping patients, the babies and their families.

One family in particular. Her reason for being here tonight. She'd been unable to stay away, even though she would have a legitimate reason to see them all in two weeks. Revenge required patience, and God, she'd waited for so long. Surely she could allow herself this small indulgence after all that had been taken from her. All the reasons she had not to trust anyone.

Milla wheeled past a janitor mopping up dried mud and stains from people tracking in wet snow, and stopped outside Naomi Steele's door. The cart held four arrangements for the new mother of twins, and a cluster of pink balloons. Milla didn't plan to make this a full-time job. It was a one-time gig with a purpose.

She hadn't been able to resist the chance to scope out the Steeles and Mikkelsons. She'd heard about the twins' birth and had conned a hospital volunteer into letting her deliver arrangements to the patients. Which technically wasn't cool on so many levels, but Milla had long ago given up playing by the rules. Life had been too harsh. She'd fought hard to build a future for herself, independent of anyone.

So she refused to feel guilty for pushing the door open and peeking inside the room. The empty room. No one lay in the bed, though the sheets were rumpled. No sounds came from the bathroom and the recliner was unoccupied.

Sighing in disappointment, she unloaded the four arrangements, placing them around the room wherever there was space—two on the window ledge, one on the rolling cart and the last by the sink. Scanning the room once more, envisioning the family that should have been in here, she tied the balloons to the end of the bed.

Her time would come. She wasn't backing down.

She had two more weeks to scope out both families before she made her move.

For years, she'd hidden out in fear of her enemies. But when she'd almost died in a wildfire last summer, she'd decided the time had arrived. She had to look out for her own safety. She'd come here to uncover the truth. The reason she'd left Canada and moved to Anchorage. To find out who was responsible for the destruction of her life—the Mikkelsons or the Steeles.

Three

Sprawled in the burgundy recliner, Royce reached overhead to stretch out his tense back. He kept his eyes trained in front of him, watching the steady rise and fall of Naomi's chest as she slept. Somehow those breaths steadied his own after the adrenaline. The fragrance of flowers throughout the room covered the antiseptic scent and reminded him of her shampoo. Her dark hair pooled around her, halo-like. Peaceful.

But this peace between them was a temporary thing. He understood that all too well.

Hospital staff had told him he could sleep on the pull-out sofa, but he'd been too restless. Once he'd texted his neighbor for an update on Tessie, he'd reached for his tablet and got to work.

The room was still dark, even though morning crept closer. Alaska days were lengthening. Naomi was tough and independent, but he hadn't thought about her handling two infant seats on an icy walkway.

Or what if she'd been trapped in that storm, alone, with the babies?

Those two tiny girls already had him wrapped around their little fingers. The breakup with Naomi had been hell, so much so he hadn't given much thought to the twins. What it would feel like to lose them. He hadn't realized how much he already cared about the two of them. That he was gutted at the thought of losing them.

Royce rubbed a crick at the back of his neck. He and Naomi had been up most of the night. The hours together reminded him of nights they'd spent in bed planning for the twins' arrival, sharing dreams for the future.

None of their discussions bore any resemblance to the way things had turned out.

Neither of them was willing to leave Anna and Mary. The pediatrician wanted them observed for the night since they'd been born early and in such unusual circumstances.

Quite frankly, Royce hadn't wanted to leave Naomi, either. Sure, her family could have stayed, but he'd seen her assert her independence with them mighty damn effectively, and hadn't trusted she would ask for help. Or that they would see what she really needed.

So he'd stayed and kicked her family out.

And yes, he'd also chosen to stick around because the glow on her face mesmerized him. The soft, soothing sound of her voice as she spoke to her babies surpassed any song.

Finally, when Naomi couldn't keep her head up any longer, a nurse had gently reminded her she would be no good to her children exhausted. She should rest while she could.

Royce had helped her back to her room and watched over her while she slept. The babies were in good hands. Someone needed to look out for Naomi. The best thing would be to walk away, but damn it all, he kept buying in to lame reasons to stick around.

He sure as hell wouldn't be able to hold off her family for long. They would all be back here en masse soon enough. For now, before the sun rose, he could imagine things were different between them.

Her feet shifted under the sheet in that way he'd learned she did just before the rest of her awoke. Back in the days when they'd shared a bed, when he'd made love to her through the night. When he'd had the right to slide his arm around her and draw her to him. To bury his face in her hair and breathe in the scent of her shampoo.

Naomi stretched her arms overhead, then swept

back her hair before gingerly sitting up in bed. "The girls?"

"Anna and Mary are fine. The nurse said they would be brought in after the shift change, which should be happening right now."

"Did you sleep at all?"

"Catnaps. I'm fine." He set his tablet aside and poured her a cup of ice water.

"Thank you." She took it and sipped. "Catnap, huh? I bet you worked."

He didn't bother denying it. The chart he'd been calculating still glowed on the screen.

"Royce, you should rest."

He could sleep later. She would be taking care of twins. "I will. How do you feel?"

"Like I gave birth to twins in a car."

"I'll get the nurse to bring your pain meds." He started to stand.

"I was joking." She gestured for him to sit again.

"Right. Guess my brain's still on stun from everything that's happened."

"Understandable." She picked at the sheets, glancing at him, then away, blinking fast. "I'm sorry if this brought back upsetting memories for you."

Yes, the delivery had brought back the past, thoughts that would haunt his sleep. But he didn't intend to worry her with that.

"My thoughts are fully on you and the babies. What about you?" He touched her hand, paused, his thumb caressing the inside of her wrist out of habit. “Is everything else, um, okay?”

“Are you referencing hormones?” She skimmed a knuckle under each eye. “Because that could be seriously dangerous to your health.”

He froze, then relaxed. “You were making a joke, right?”

“Teasing you.” She squinted, sizing him up with a playful grin. “Not a joke exactly.”

“Got it.” He tapped his temple, missing this ease between them, not knowing how to keep it beyond sunrise. “I’m working on developing a sense of humor.”

“You’ve always had one. You’re just more literal when you’re stressed.” She bit her lip. “I’m sorry you had to go through that.”

The pain in her words cut him to the quick. “There’s nothing for you to apologize for.”

“And yes, to answer your question, I’m thinking about my mom and my sister.” She shrugged, the green hospital gown sliding down one shoulder. “I wish they were here to see the girls, to offer advice. Just to hug.”

He covered her hand with his, stroking lightly.

Ah, there it was. An old familiar spark. The feeling of an electric current running between them, gaining voltage as her eyes caught his.

Memories catapulted through his mind, threatening to tear down the wall between them.

But the moment was short-lived, interrupted by

a squeaky hospital door. Back to the present. To the babies being lifted out of the bassinets and into the arms of the nurse.

A cooing noise erupted from the pink lips of one of the girls as the nurse carefully cradled the tiny pink bundle.

"Are you ready, Momma?" the woman asked brightly, her ponytail swinging as she moved closer.

Naomi's heart was in her eyes as she looked at the nurse and nodded emphatically, her dark hair tumbling forward.

Damn.

Naomi practically glowed with maternal love and happiness. The sight of her reaching for her babies, cradling one and then the other to her chest, nearly knocked him to his knees.

"Are you sure you have them?" the nurse inquired, propping pillows under Naomi's arms to give her support.

Two babies, even at this young age, were a lot to juggle. Royce hovered. Wanting to help.

Needing to help.

"I'll make sure," he answered the nurse, easing past her to give Naomi a hand.

Seeing for himself how much she needed help meant only one thing. He had to be there for her these next six weeks as she recovered and settled into motherhood, or he would never be free of regrets.

* * *

Naomi wrapped baby Anna in her blanket, swaddling her the way the nurses had taught. Mary already slept, her sweet Cupid's bow mouth moving silently as she dreamed. So far nursing the twins was going well. At least that's what the staff said. Naomi found it more difficult than she'd expected, but she was determined to try.

It had taken all her skills as a lawyer to convince Royce to step out of the room long enough to visit the cafeteria. She'd convinced him she had to have a burger.

She carefully adjusted the pink cap on Anna and the purple cap on Mary before relaxing in the recliner by her bed. Sitting in a real chair made her feel more like a regular person after all the weeks on bed rest before she gave birth. And after the ordeal of doing so in the SUV. Usually, Naomi thrived on drama and high emotions. But was it too much to ask to have a second of peace without all these feelings crowding her? She'd given birth in a freaking car. She deserved—her babies deserved—a few minutes of calm.

The reactions stirred by Royce were anything but peaceful.

She knew the two of them were over. They had to be. They weren't good for each other. It had just been infatuation. But he still sent her hormones into a tailspin whenever he walked in the room.

And when he walked out. Even to go get supper.

What would it feel like when he left forever?

As the lump in her throat swelled to an almost unmanageable size—so much for peace—the door cracked open.

Again, anticipation hummed in her veins, made her heart race—*hope*—to see the eccentric scientist appear.

And yes, there was a man in the entry. But it wasn't Royce.

Her rugged father, an unwavering—albeit gruff—teddy bear of support through the years. He carried a vase of pink roses.

"Daddy? I can't believe you're here." She pushed on the arms of the recliner to stand.

With a hand on her shoulder, he gently eased her back, then wedged the painted ceramic vase on the counter between a spider plant and a pair of rag dolls. "Of course I'm here to see my girl and her babies. Jeannie's here, too. She's just outside the door with the family. She said I should have some time alone with you first. She's thoughtful that way. Always trying to be considerate when it comes to the blending of our families."

Naomi shifted to face him as he pulled up another chair to sit beside her. She was happy for her father, truly, but right now, with an ache in her heart from wanting her mother to share this moment, it was difficult to think about her father's remarriage. Selfish of her? Probably. But emotions weren't easy and she'd always been the volatile one in the family.

Still, she tried her diplomatic best for her dad. "I didn't mean to bring you back from your honeymoon."

"We wouldn't miss this for anything. I want to hold my granddaughters once they wake up." He peered into each bassinet, touching the newborns' tiny caps reverently. "Lordy, girl, they're beautiful."

"I won't disagree with you there." Love filled her heart for these two lives. The swell of emotion was so deep and wide she could barely contain it.

"I had to push my way to the front of the line. There's quite a train of people out there waiting to see these little ones." He paused, eyeing her. "I saw Royce on my way in. Are you two back togeth—"

Swiftly, she held up her hand, cutting him off. "No, Dad." She didn't have the strength to fight rumors or explain yet again why they'd broken up, especially not now when her emotions were turning somersaults inside her. She could repeat only so many times that they were just too different. Sharing anything more about their breakup felt too personal, even to tell her family. "He just happened to be there when the babies were born."

"How so, exactly?" Jack narrowed his brows, his weathered face furrowing.

Hadn't he heard? Of course he would have questioned the others. She searched her father's face and decided this was another battle not worth fighting. He clearly wanted to hear her side, to see if she was weakening in reuniting with her ex-fiancé—who also happened to be her father's new golden boy consultant in the company.

Fine. "Royce took me to my OB appointment, where I got a glowing report, so good I was let off bed rest. Then we drove around for a while to celebrate. We talked about heading to Kit's Kodiak Café, because I had a craving for their Three Polar Bears special—"

"Like when you were a kid. I look forward to taking the girls there one day, along with Fleur." Broderick and Glenna's toddler. "This grandpa gig is a good thing. Now finish telling me how these nuggets entered the world in Royce's car."

"While we were out, it began snowing. Labor started…and the next thing I knew, I was giving birth on the side of the road in his Suburban." She grimaced.

Her dad chuckled. "I was there when each of you were born, you know." His eyes took on a nostalgic glint for a moment before he blinked it away.

"Please say you're going to finish your trip, though."

"Jeannie and I want to welcome you home first. Then we'll fly back out and resume the rest of our belated honeymoon."

Exhausted and emotional, Naomi inwardly winced at the thought of a big to-do. She loved her family and would need their support. Still, she yearned for bonding time with her daughters.

Even so, being a parent now gave her a new perspective on her father, and she didn't want to hurt his feelings. So she simply smiled and said, "That sounds perfect. I'll be sure to send you lots of photos of the babies."

He fished his smartphone out of his jeans pocket, waved it in the air with a wide, bright smile. "Please do. I'll be passing my phone around for everyone to see."

"You'll be back before you know it for your big wedding party." Her father and Jeannie had been married in a small service with all their children present, but given their business connections, they'd planned for a large gala after they returned from their honeymoon. After which the pipeline modifications would kick into high gear, as would Royce's workload.

"The twins will be six weeks old then." His face took on a nostalgic air as he traced the edges of the pink cap. "Little Anna here looks like you."

"Or like Breanna, you mean."

He nodded, his throat bobbing, his gaze still locked on the newborn.

"Are you sure you're all right with the names?" Naomi squeezed her father's forearm. "I don't want you to feel sad when you see them."

"I'm happy. I mean it. Seeing these two little granddaughters reminds me of my twins in all the best ways." He scrubbed his wrist across his eyes, a wide smile replacing any pain that had been on his face. "Thank you, Naomi."

"I love you, Dad." She leaned across the arm of the chair to hug him.

He folded her into a familiar embrace, patting her back rhythmically, like…a dad. "Love you, too." Finally, he angled away, standing. "Now I'm going to get Jeannie before she goes crazy waiting."

That brief sadness on her father's face and in his voice made Naomi's heart ache more than she could remember since she'd been a teenager. Scared. Unsure of the future.

Well, except for when she'd broken things off with Royce. She could still remember the shock on his face, the denial. She hadn't been able to handle his smothering, his lack of understanding when it came to her need for independence, his unwillingness to acknowledge her strength. She realized he responded that way because of his former fiancée's miscarriage, but still, Naomi had fought too hard to climb out of the cocoon her family had put her in during her bout with cancer.

Royce had accused her of being so stuck in the past she was afraid to embrace the future.

Likely they both had valid points, but bottom line, they'd jumped into the relationship too quickly.

That didn't make the breakup hurt less.

He was a good man. Almost too good—if there could be such a thing. Even while she realized theirs had been an infatuation—a hefty dose of infatuation—she'd known without question he never would have broken things off with her once he'd committed to be there for her, for her children. That honorable nature had made it all the tougher for her to do the right thing and let him go.

She rubbed at the sore spot on her wrist where the IV had been, the lingering ache reminding her of so many other pains, losses.

Royce could sit and crunch numbers, work equations and create charts for hours without feeling the least bit drained. He liked to think he had grit and stamina by the bucketful. But a day spent with inquiring and nervous family members reminded him of another skill he had to work on—resilience. Tension in his jaw conveyed his overexposure. But it was worth it for Naomi and the babies.

She was washing her hair. The sound of the showering water through the door had soothed the girls to sleep. He had to admit to being moved when Naomi had trusted him with them after her family left for supper.

The Steele-Mikkelsons never ceased to surprise him. Such as how this family worth billions, who'd wined and dined with world leaders, still chose Kit's Kodiak Café as one of their favorite watering holes. Sure, the food rocked, but he thought maybe it fit more with their pace, all of them having grown up near oil fields.

They were used to a big clan, but he was more comfortable in the solitude of his cabin with his dog Naomi had sensed that, no matter how hard he'd tried to hide it. And he had tried, because he'd wanted things to work between them.

He'd failed. And no amount of Mensa IQ points could help him figure out how to fix things so they worked together as a couple.

But that wasn't the task at hand.

Instead he'd create a perfect system that would enable a smooth transition for her and the girls. Rather than second-guessing every waking moment, he'd enjoy his time with Naomi, help situate her for success in the future.

Goals and objectives. Now he had something to work for—to help Naomi—and even a deadline. He would be there for her until her father's return from his honeymoon.

Royce made his way to the curious-eyed infants, who blinked up at him, stealing their way deeper into his heart.

"Hello, beautiful girls," he said softly. Anna crinkled her nose at the sound of his voice. "Did you know that matter is never destroyed, only converted? We have to make sure you two are at the top of your class. Yeah-huh."

A female doctor with a gray ballerina bun entered the room, cutting the science lesson short. He turned to face her, and the male nurse with a crew cut who followed, introducing themselves. Her regular OB, Dr. Odell, had gone on vacation, so his partner was making rounds.

"She's in the shower," Royce explained, just before the water stopped. "But as you can hear, she's finishing up."

"That's fine. We're about to undergo a shift change, but are also in the process of releasing patients that are able to be discharged this evening."

"Oh. Well, uh, I'm not sure how she feels."

"That's quite all right. We can wait to ask her." The doctor gestured to the darkening window. "Full moon tonight. And that means a lot of women in labor."

Naomi emerged from the bathroom in a plush pink robe and nightgown, looking pretty with her hair gathered in a damp braid.

The doctor smiled, shifting her clipboard from one hand to the other. "Well, Momma, I am prepared to release you—if you feel comfortable, that is."

Relief flooded her face. "Yes, please. I would like to go home."

Home. Royce's gut clenched. There'd been a time when they'd shared his house, talked of buying a larger place with space for the babies. That scenario had passed.

The doctor pushed her glasses up the bridge of her nose, then passed the clipboard to the nurse. "I'll have him start your discharge paperwork. You have infant car seats?"

Naomi pointed toward the corner. "My family brought them today."

"Good, good." The nurse penciled a check mark

on the papers before tucking the clipboard under his arm.

The doctor touched each baby's head lightly before squeezing Naomi's shoulder. "We have plenty of guides and emergency numbers in your baby welcome packet. Don't hesitate to call if you have any questions."

The nurse pulled the papers off the clipboard and tucked them into a sack with the hospital logo on the side. "Congratulations. To both of you. All four of you, actually. I never grow jaded about the joy of releasing a family."

A family. Royce didn't bother correcting the nurse. He'd actually given up on correcting that assumption at all—and apparently so had Naomi—after the second shift change had brought in yet another wave of well-wishers who assumed he was the father.

"Wow, I can't believe we're leaving. It's all happening so fast." She opened the cabinet and pulled out the clothes her sister had brought. "Thank goodness Delaney brought a bag for the babies and me. And their car seats."

"Lucky to have all that here. Makes things easier. Although you could wear your boots with the nightgown and coat. No need to tire yourself out." He couldn't miss the furrows creasing her forehead. "Naomi?"

She shook her head, pulling out the loose sweater dress. "It's just a little overwhelming. Not the way I envisioned it. Although I will go home in this, like I planned."

"Right. And I'll get the girls in those little outfits you picked out for them." At least he hoped he could. Figuring out how to build modifications for a safer, more efficient oil pipeline sounded easier at the moment than wrangling those spindly baby arms into miniscule matching clothes. "Take your time getting dressed. I'll be sure to snap plenty of photos. Your girls are going home. You're a mom."

Going still, she held the dress against her, her eyes sad again, in that way that twisted him up inside.

"Naomi? What's wrong?"

Her mouth opened and closed twice before she finally blurted out, "I know there was a time when you opened your heart to be their father. I realize this can't be easy for you. You can come see them if you wish."

And just that fast, the thoughts that had been churning in his head all day took shape into a plan. An unwavering sense of direction. He shoved aside her concerns that he was just filling a void in his life. They weren't a couple anymore, but he could still do this for her. "Oh, I'm going to be seeing plenty of the girls and of you."

"Um, what?" She angled her head to the side, her damp braid swishing forward.

Maybe he should have waited until later to tell her, once he pulled up at the Steele compound and unloaded her and the girls in Naomi's suite of rooms. But hopefully the car ride would give her a chance to settle into the idea.

Or give him more time to convince her he wasn't budging.

"Because for the next six weeks, I'm moving in to be your nanny."

Four

This place was a sight for sore eyes. Or rather more accurately, a sore heart.

In her family's six-bay garage, Naomi cast a glance at Royce, the silent giant who'd taken over her life.

For a man who wanted solitude, he'd sure thrown himself into the fire, signing on to be here with her girls and her family. She had help. Sure, they all worked and she didn't want to impose. But she had a wide support system.

Yet she hadn't been able to tell him no. She needed to know what was really behind this crazy offer of his to be the girls' temporary nanny.

She fumbled with the diaper bag, trying to remain

as quiet as possible. Waking up the sleeping babies fell low on her list of things to do. The massive garage ran the entire length of the back of the house, and sounds tended to reverberate off the top-of-the-line SUVs and snowmobiles in the space.

Exhaustion gnawed on her as she made her way around the SUV Royce had rented. Royce. A nanny. *Her* nanny. For better or worse.

"Royce," Naomi whispered, shrugging her damp braid over her shoulder. "Just so we're clear, this is temporary. Tonight only, because it took us so much longer to sign out of the hospital than I expected—and longer again to get here with the sleet outside. I don't want to wake up my family. If they all roll out of bed, it will be forever before we can get to sleep."

And she knew she was making excuses, but as far as excuses went, it was a solid one.

He simply nodded, hefting both baby car seats and then shouldering the vehicle doors closed. Anna snoozed on, but Mary flinched in her seat. Royce froze.

Naomi didn't dare breathe.

With a tiny sigh, Mary settled back to sleep again.

Naomi picked her way down the hall, making sure they didn't disturb the sleeping household. She could practically do the walk to her room in her sleep. The familiar path was as natural to her as breathing. She led him up the stairs, past a great gallery wall of childhood photographs. A repository for all that was familiar.

But as she approached the elevator to her suite, she noticed more photographs. New ones, of Jeannie and her family. Naomi's world was expanding and fracturing all at once.

She heard a voice drifting softly from the study. Her sister's voice. Someone was awake, after all. Naomi could send Royce on his way.

The disappointment hit her hard, right in her riotous hormones.

Then Birch Montoya's voice joined Delaney's. The man was a new investor in their family's oil company, a shark who had butted heads with Delaney on her environmental concerns. "You don't have to disagree with everything I propose."

"Well, Birch…" Delaney's voice rose. "If any of it showed a care about the environment, then I wouldn't argue."

Royce's eyebrows shot up. He tipped his head toward the home elevator leading to her suite. Naomi eyed the door to the library where her sister was working…

Or rather arguing. Loudly. She looked over at the babies, then up at Royce. And she couldn't deny she was using the argument behind that library door as an excuse to do exactly what she wanted.

To spend this first night playing house with Royce.

Royce adjusted his grip on the car seats, evaluating the weight of the babies. How strange it felt to hold them as he moved into Naomi's suite. How silent the elevator ride had been, his head filled with memories of a time he'd expected to bring his own child home. Plans and dreams made. Nightmares that followed. And lingered.

He rubbed his bleary eyes to clear his thoughts. He needed to keep a level head and be present for Naomi. He'd half expected her to call her family to drive to the hospital to transport her and the twins, but the lengthy checkout time, lateness of the hour and desire to go home had apparently won out.

A nursery had been added to the suite since he'd been here last. Gray and pink accent colors surprised him, though the logical part of his mind knew there'd have to be an addition made to her living quarters. Still, the newness caught him off guard. The babies' room hadn't been here when they'd broken up. When he'd left here for the last time.

Back when he'd stayed here, the nursery had been an enclosed balcony where he and Naomi had spent a lot of hours together talking. And more.

Now, two pewter-colored cribs flanked a plush glider. Bookshelves were decorated with overstuffed toys and tons of books. There was no trace of their former life.

Did she think of those times anymore?

Better not to think of the past at all. Best to focus on the future.

He turned away from the nursery and thought of how this coming home could have been so very different. Peering into the car seats, he saw that the twins still slept. Good. He made his way to the double bassinet in Naomi's room, where the girls would sleep for the time being. "I'm going to run down and get the rest of your luggage."

And a bag he'd packed for himself.

"Are you sure you don't mind? I feel like I'm imposing."

"I wouldn't have offered if I minded. I'll be right back."

He jogged down the steps, finding all quiet in the waterside mansion. Unusual, to say the least. Even the study had gone silent. Birch and Delaney must have settled their argument. The two were at constant loggerheads. Birch kept his focus on the company's financial bottom line. Delaney had her eye solidly on protecting the environment.

Royce entered the garage and pulled the two cases from the rented SUV, then turned to head back to Naomi's suite, where he'd once stayed overnight often. But now they'd grown so far apart she hadn't even shown him the nursery.

Shuffling one of the bags under his arm, he reentered, elbowing the door closed again behind him.

Returning to Naomi's quarters, he found her bent over the bassinet. Her dark hair fell in waves, an aftershock of her earlier braids. The glossy silk framed her radiant face as she watched Mary sleeping. Cradling Anna in her arms, she rocked back and forth, hips seeming to glide against the fresh sea green nightgown.

A pull of familiarity. Of normalcy.

Being together this way was almost like they'd once imagined the aftermath of the girls' birth. Well, except they'd planned to have their own house and be married. So really, not much that mattered was the same.

Naomi eased into her glider chair and toed it into slow motion, patting Anna's back. "The house is so quiet. I guess Delaney and Birch must have finished up their work."

"Do you want me to get your sister?"

"No, don't bother her. Everyone else will wake up and… Honestly, I prefer this to a big to-do. There will be plenty of attention in the morning. I'll be more rested then." She looked at the babies. "Well, I know they'll have me up through the night, but at least I won't have the nurses coming in all the time, too."

"I'm here to help you as much as you need. You know that." He wondered what her family would say when they saw him in the morning.

What did he want them to say? To think? Damned if he knew, beyond figuring out some way to settle the raw, torn-apart feeling between them. Neither of them could continue working together this way.

"For tonight. Just tonight. That nanny business was a cute line, but really?"

"Really. We shared an intense time, and you

know as well as I do there hasn't been…closure. We still have to work together."

"Closure, huh? That's what this is about?"

"What else would it be about?"

She stared at him through narrowed eyes before finally shaking her head, then yawning, her hand over her mouth.

"I'm too tired to discuss this any longer. Thank you for the help tonight so I didn't have to impose on my family more than I'm already going to be imposing these next few months." Her face changed from exhaustion to something lighter, happier as she put Anna down in her bassinet. She lingered over her child for a moment before turning to face Royce.

The weariness flooded her eyes again as she looked above him to the ceiling, wooden beams stretching the width of the room. "You and I can talk in the morning right before you go back to your place."

"Uh-huh." He checked Mary in the other bassinet, watching the even rise and fall of her chest, avoiding Naomi's reference to the morning.

Naomi cleared her throat softly. "I'm not going to be distracted."

He wished he knew a way to dissolve all the tension between them. Royce pulled back the comforter on her bed before cupping her shoulders, fighting the urge to linger, to stroke his thumbs along the silky skin of her neck. "Rest."

"Why is it I win in the courtroom—" she sighed,

sinking to rest on the edge of the mattress "—but you always manage to outtalk me with just a handful of words?"

"Not always."

Her eyes filled with sorrow and she clasped his wrist. "I'm sorry."

"Me, too." And he was. He just didn't know how to fix things. And he sure as hell didn't want to move her hand from him. He'd missed her touch. More than he'd realized.

She eased her hand away, clenching her fist in her lap. "I still feel I'm being selfish in keeping you here."

"I wouldn't be here if I didn't want to be." He patted the pillow. "Are you going to use this bed? Because if not, I will be more than happy to sack out—"

Chuckling, she swung her feet up. "Fine. And thank you again for everything."

"You're welcome. I'll be right out there on the sofa if you need me."

She sat up straighter, winced, then said, "On the sofa? So you really mean to stay the nights here, too?"

"I'm a very dedicated nanny." He grasped the door handle. "Now sleep."

No one had warned Naomi how exhausted she'd be after giving birth. Okay, maybe people had, but she clearly hadn't grasped the full depth of the bone-weary feeling that would overwhelm her. A part of her wondered if the fatigue came from her exposure to Royce. To that future she'd missed out on when their relationship fell apart.

Despite all that, she managed to sit at the breakfast table with her family, take in all the chatter like it was just another average day.

Delaney held Mary, while Glenna and Broderick introduced their daughter, Fleur, to her new cousin Anna. The rest of her family made diplomatic small talk at the other end of the table—and avoided mentioning the fact that Royce had filled a plate of food and gone back upstairs with the excuse he needed to catch up on work. She saw well enough how the crowded dining room made the corner of one of his eyes tic.

The night had been a blur of waking up to feed the babies, then falling asleep again, only to wake up what felt like seconds later. Royce had been such a help throughout, making things go faster by changing and burping each girl while she fed the other.

"Did you and Birch settle the work issues last night?"

Delaney looked up fast, then set her fork down slowly, Mary cradled in her other arm. "What do you mean?"

"I wasn't eavesdropping, but when I got home last night I couldn't help but hear the two of you arguing, something to do with business."

"You shouldn't have to worry about the office

right now. Just focus on recovering and enjoying those adorable babies."

Naomi waved her hand dismissively, then tapped her temple. "I still have a brain—albeit an exhausted one. I care about the family business. And I feel guilty that so much is falling on your shoulders."

"Glenna and Broderick are helping. And Trystan Mikkelson has been a surprise thanks to Isabeau's good influence. I bet fatherhood smooths those rough edges on him even more." Delaney picked her fork up again to chase food around her plate.

"I just want to make sure our interests are protected."

"You'll be back at the office soon enough." Delaney shot her sister a sidelong glance.

"And are you sure things are okay? He can be quite…a shark."

"I have a handle on him." Delaney refilled her china coffee cup and set down the silver carafe, leaning forward to whisper, "What about you and Royce?"

Loaded question. With all the calmness she could muster, Naomi said in a flat voice, "He says he plans to be the nanny for the next six weeks."

Delaney's eyes went wide, and she placed Mary carefully in the portable bassinet, her attention now 100 percent on Naomi. "Nanny?"

"I know, right?" Shoveling some scrambled egg into her mouth, she bought herself some time before talking. "The breakup was difficult for both of us. I think he sees this as closure. Or obligation to the babies. That's been a worry all along, actually. I figure he will give up in a week. Two weeks tops. The lure of a full night's sleep with no diaper changes will win."

Even thinking of him walking away hurt.

"Maybe," Delaney said skeptically.

"Definitely."

"It's romantic that he offered."

Naomi's heart thudded in her chest, painfully so. "There's no romance. I just had twins. And I did deliver them right in front of him." Now that the rush of the moment had passed, she couldn't help but feel…embarrassed? Unveiled? "It's different somehow than if he'd just been there holding my hand in the delivery room."

Although he had been mighty amazing, considering the situation. A rock.

"Romance is about more than sex." Her sister sounded very definite about it.

"I know that." And in some ways, that's what made Naomi the saddest about the breakup with Royce. Wondering if all they'd had was physical. That her heart had been so…confused by attraction. She considered herself a woman of logic and she'd been led by her libido.

"Just checking."

In spite of everything, something spurred her to blurt, "The sex was really good, though."

"Then I guess it's a lucky thing you can't be

tempted by Royce, since you're looking at six weeks of postpartum recovery." Delaney raised the coffee cup to her lips, appearing utterly unconvinced.

"Thanks for the reminder I have a flabby body and lactating breasts. Definitely not a temptation for him." More of that embarrassment stung her.

"That's not what I said. I meant that this is a time the two of you can get to know each other better—without sex clouding the issue like it did before, when you two jumped into a relationship too fast."

"That sounds judgy."

"Trust me, I'm the last one to pass judgment on that subject." Delaney attacked the food on her plate.

Naomi tried to read her sister's expression, but that was tough to do when she kept her eyes averted. Interesting. "Delaney? Do you have something to share to distract me from the fact that I'm exhausted and my former fiancé has moved in to be my temporary nanny?"

She glanced up, a blush spreading across her cheeks. "Nothing."

Apparently there was more than one person keeping secrets in this family. "The least you could do is help distract me from my exhaustion and wrecked love life with some juicy tidbits from your world."

Delaney crinkled her nose. "Nothing to share," she insisted, clearly lying. "How about we cuddle these adorable babies of yours some more? By far the most interesting event going on right now."

Naomi relented, unable to argue with people

pouring love out for her children. She reached into the bassinet by the table and passed Anna to Delaney.

Seemed that everyone had secrets and a love life.

And Naomi had a sexy male nanny she couldn't sleep with who only wanted her for her babies.

Five

When Royce signed on for the nanny gig two weeks ago, he hadn't expected that would take them to the Steele corporate headquarters with the twins in tow.

Naomi had gotten an emergency call from the office asking for information to deal with a handful of crises. He could see how torn she was between work and her children, so he'd suggested taking the babies to the workplace, where he would help with them while she handled business.

The relief on her face had been so intense he managed to stifle frustration over having to trudge with her to the company headquarters. With luck, he could use the opportunity to throw in some hints about the benefits of a home office. Absolutely his preferred work environment.

Naomi was using Glenna's desk, since her sister-in-law was working from home today. The space was also larger than Naomi's—and already stocked with baby gear for Glenna's daughter. The setup surprised Royce, but then he'd made a point to spend as little time as possible here, doing his research off site and coming in only for boardroom reports.

How was it that he'd spent so little time in Naomi's workplace?

Royce held Anna against his shoulder, patting her back, while Naomi nursed Mary and handled her business call simultaneously. She'd already addressed legal issues with firing an employee. Then she'd scanned documents from some drama-causing Florida investor.

None of which could have been easy, since Glenna's assistant had retired and the replacement had only just started. Naomi's assistant was out for major surgery, so she and Glenna were sharing.

So much upheaval, yet Naomi made it all look effortless.

She was such a dynamo. A mesmerizing dynamo.

"Dwight," she said into the phone, patient but firm, "the contracts were emailed a month ago, with hard copies sent, as well. You were out of the office for quite a while before I went on maternity leave." She paused, nodding her head, her lips getting tighter. “I only received your questions today. So let’s work on addressing them—”

She went silent again as the voice on the other end of the phone rose, talking faster. Ranting. Naomi tucked the phone between her ear and shoulder and passed the baby over to Royce, mouthing *thank you*.

Balancing a now sleeping Anna, he set her down in the work space crib. The little girl stretched out slightly, reaching as if to yank on his heartstrings. He placed drowsy Mary in the white crib beside her sister, her little fingers curled into something that looked like a wave. One that could sweep right over him too easily.

He walked to one of the white sofas, settling into the surprisingly firm cushion. The wall of windows showcased the autumn sky. He’d thought nothing could be more majestic than a Texas landscape—until he’d come to Alaska.

Light snow coated the mountaintops in the distance, beautiful, regal. Just like the woman in this office who juggled motherhood while putting out legal fires as if she’d been managing the combination for years. He glanced back at Naomi just as she absently shook her head again, the echoing buzz of Dwight’s voice still filling the silence.

Finally, the ass on the other end of the line seemed to run out of steam.

Naomi adjusted the phone against her ear. “I hear your concerns. Loud and clear. We can address them calmly at four o’clock this afternoon, eastern time, when I've had time to consult at length with the rest of the legal team." Her voice was all business, leaving no room for argument. "At which time you can decide if you wish to complete this deal and be a part of Alaska Oil Barons' ecofriendly pipeline to the Dakotas—along with all of the positive press that entails. Or you are welcome to roll the dice with Johnson Oil."

Cal Johnson was in a tailspin over his competition's upgrades. Even Johnson's CEO, Ward Benally, had resigned. And clearly Naomi knew this gave her an edge to use.

Royce couldn't help but think of the day they'd met, when she'd tracked him down to a remote cabin to persuade him to share his research with her family's company. He'd been skeptical about joining Alaska Oil Barons, but the Steeles and the Mikkelsons had proved themselves to be strong advocates for his vision. He appreciated the fire and conviction in her voice.

Whatever Dwight said brought a victorious smile to Naomi's face. She nodded, then said, "Glad to hear you're feeling reassured. And yes, tomorrow is fine with me, since you're busy this afternoon. Happy to accommodate. Have a nice rest of your day. We'll speak soon."

She disconnected the call and exhaled hard. "Jerk."

"He's a jerk who apparently lost whatever edge he expected to gain."

Her fingers lingered on a glass swan figurine that looked as if it were carved from ice. Steel entered her voice as she straightened papers on Glenna's desk, then swiveled in the plush black chair. "He deserves to lose a lot more."

"I agree." Royce let his gaze wander from her angled face. Natural sunlight filtered into the office, framing her at the desk between the two towering bookshelves behind her. "Your firm sense of right and wrong is very attractive."

Damn, but she mesmerized him. Loose waves of her hair gathered just above her breasts, feathering out against her flowy blue dress. She stood, moving around the desk, her leather boots softly pressing into the off-white carpet.

"Thank you." She smiled, her cheeks pink, color returning to her face after being pale for a few days. "And thank you for pitching in with the babies so I could take care of this problem. I hope I'm not taking advantage and detracting from your own work?"

"Nothing to worry about. I took some time off from lecturing at the university. And flexibility is the benefit of being a consultant. I can set my own schedule, plus any tweaks to the current project with the pipeline can be done remotely while the babies sleep." The success of his patents afforded him the luxury of never working again if he so chose. Not that he saw himself ever retiring. He enjoyed inventing, helping the work, and delivering the occasional college seminar to teach future generations. All of which left him with the creative freedom to pursue research grants as inspiration struck.

"Regardless," she said, "you've gone above and beyond. And I have to admit, it was helpful to have the paperwork in front of me today."

"You could have things couriered to the house."

"I could have..." She scrunched her nose, exhaling as she made her way to the sofa. She sat on the arm of the adjacent couch, looked over her shoulder to the window. Naomi took a deep breath before turning to face him. "Okay, truth? I needed to get out of the house and this was the perfect excuse. Thank you for helping make it happen in a way I didn't have to worry about the girls."

Coming here hadn't been as much of a chore as he'd initially thought. The stillness of the office surprised him. Solitude seemed to settle in the room—the kind he craved, and the kind that didn't permeate the Steele family compound. Attraction heightened in the solitude.

Royce cleared his throat, needing a physical act to disrupt his intense eye contact with Naomi. Eye contact that reawakened all sorts of desires in him. He needed to pull on his professional skills to help him now. "I meant it when I said I wanted to help... and before you go ballistic, wondering if I'm trying to use the twins as a replacement family, let's just settle on a compromise. You and I both have issues to work through. And in letting me help you, you're helping me."

"You make that sound too easy. There has to be a catch." Naomi moved from her perch to sit next to him.

"Quit thinking like a lawyer."

She sagged into the couch, her skirt pooling around her knees, exposing her shapely calves. "A tired lawyer. Thank goodness Dwight didn't take me up on my offer to get everything together today."

"The girls are sleeping, so let's not risk waking them up by carrying them down to the car." He touched the small of her back, and damn, but the familiar feel of her soaked right into him. Not that anything could happen between them. She'd broken his heart. He was here for closure, not to fall back into old patterns of leaning on their sensual connection.

Clearing his throat again, he pulled his hand away and motioned to one of the sofas. "Stretch out on the couch, put your feet up and eat something. I have to confess, I wouldn't mind doing the same."

"You've been too kind to me."

"We have to work together. Unless you want me to quit consulting—"

"Bite your tongue. My family would kill me."

Chuckling, he settled onto the sofa across from her and studied the coffee table sporting a platter of food they'd ordered up from the headquarters' five-star restaurant. He loaded up a plate from the antipasto selection of cured meats, cheeses, olives, crostinis and a fruit spread. "Well, we can't have that."

She plucked an olive from the plate he handed her and nibbled it.

"What are you thinking?" he asked, trying to ignore the low buzz of his phone with an incoming text.

"Just remembering some old times. This was a favorite snack when we were kids—minus the olives back then." She swung her feet up onto the sofa, sitting up against throw pillows with her plate of food. "Life was so idyllic before the accident. Camping trips. Family dinners. And yes, it was noisy, but so happy. Even when we weren't getting along, it was funny, because it wasn't mean-spirited. Does that make sense?"

"Knowing your family? Yes." Having grown up an only child, he was intrigued by their dynamics, the ability to coexist in a crowd.

"Marshall and Brea loved trekking in snowshoes."

"I'm assuming from the tone in your voice that you didn't feel the same?" His phone buzzed again and he checked quickly, finding a work text that could wait. He switched off his cell and turned his attention to Naomi.

"I wanted to curl up with a book at the cabin."

"Seriously? You wanted to be alone?" He couldn't resist teasing her on that count.

"I wasn't totally alone. My grandmother was there—my mother's mom. She said she stayed at the cabin in case one of us kids needed to come back, but she had COPD and couldn't handle the long walks anymore. I cherished the time alone with her, not competing with the others."

"She was a strong influence in your life."

"I don't know what I would have done without her when I went through cancer treatments. I don't know how she held so strong so soon after her daughter—my mom—died." Naomi looked over at the crib with her sleeping babies. "I can't even imagine the pain she must have felt. But she was there for me. Telling me endless stories in the hospital. I can still hear the sound of her voice."

"What kinds of stories?"

Naomi smiled more to herself than to Royce. Her eyes took on a faraway, nostalgic look, and suddenly he found himself even more invested in their conversation.

"My grandmother made sure we heard the legends directly from her, not from a book. Like the tale of the Qalupalik—one of our favorites. She was green and slimy and lived in the water. She hummed and would draw bad children to the waves. If you wandered away from your parents, she would slip you in a pouch on her back and take you to her watery home to live with her other kids. You would never see your family again."

"Your grandma sounds like a tough cookie."

"She was. That story actually used to scare all of us to pieces when we were younger. Delaney cried the first time she heard it. But then the story was familiar and a part of our ritual."

He saw something lurking in her eyes that prompted him to ask, "What were some of your other favorite stories?"

"There's also the werewolf legend about the Adlet. They were said to have the lower body of a wolf and the upper body of a human—"

"Like centaurs," Royce said, before biting into a slice of sharp cheese.

"Basically, yes. And apparently, they still roam. Broderick and Marshall tried to hunt one once. They had to turn back because I tagged along, and Aiden followed me..." She straightened, setting her plate down on the couch cushion beside her. She tensed and Royce could practically see the walls fly up as her voice took on a decidedly more defensive tone. "Are you just being polite? You have to have heard all of this about the werewolf legend. It's a well-known one."

"I haven't heard it this way. Not from you." She narrowed her eyes as if trying to discern his intent. "What are you trying to tell me?"

"Marshall and Brea were always close. People worried more about him after we lost her, and I understand that. But she and I were close, too." A pained smile tugged at her mouth. "She was my sister. I was supposed to protect her."

"Naomi, you were still a kid. That's a heavy burden to put on yourself."

"I know that in my mind, but in my heart?" She blinked back tears. "Since my sister Brea died, it seems like the family is missing a part—like the Adlet legend."

"It's understandable that she's on your mind now."

"I keep thinking about how my girls will never know her."

Ah, hell. Objectivity and distance weren't even an option. He set aside his plate and moved to the other sofa. He shifted her until he could pull her against his side and hold her. She didn't resist. In fact, a shuddering sigh went through her that rocked him to his core.

They both grew silent and he stroked her hair, breathing in the scent of *her*. Every breath pulled temptation tauter inside him.

Her curves molded to his side, the swell of her breasts a sweet temptation. She was drifting off, but he was very much wide-awake. Her breathing eventually slowed even as his heartbeat thudded harder in his ears. And lower.

Sitting here, holding her, was torturous. Apparently, he was a masochist, because he couldn't bring himself to move.

Gathering bottles into a black diaper bag with polar bears stitched on the handles, Naomi took a moment to breathe. And man, did she need to after the last hour of her life.

Having Royce nearby had been a godsend. She

moved through work, felt less wiped out than the day before. But she needed to get out, away from the sweet domesticity of playing house with Royce. Dividing up the tasks also made transitioning into her professional life infinitely easier.

But as for her heart? Another matter entirely.

This time with Royce had been too enticing. Too much like things were before, except with two sleeping infants in the room.

Well, and the fact that they couldn't have sex.

Which, now that she thought about it, actually made today different from before, since they'd spent most of their past jumping into bed together. Often. So why was he sticking around?

The obvious answer stung all over again. That he was looking for a replacement family. Or closure for that lost family.

Her heart hurt—and a fierce protective feeling flowed through Naomi. Her children would be no one's replacement.

She would not stay this vulnerable. No. She needed to channel her last name. Erect those famous "Steele" walls.

She quickened her pace, searching the room for any lingering toys and necessities. At this point, Naomi felt she was almost on autopilot. She barely registered Royce's presence. Or perhaps more accurately, tried to ignore the way he attentively searched the room for stray items.

He placed a hand on her shoulder, the warmth both familiar and new. That was confusing.

"Hey, slow down, Naomi. I've got it. You've done a lot today on your first big day out, other than for a doctor's visit."

He moved closer, the musky scent of him reminding her of the bed that they once shared while making love for hours on end. What it was like to be with him, their bodies slick with sweat and need. Then afterward, sated, resting her head on his muscled chest, listening to the heavy slug of his heart against his ribs.

The memory made her move faster as she stepped away, under the guise of picking up a throw pillow off the floor and replacing it on the sofa. "I'm fine. I'll be home soon with plenty of family to help."

There. Take the hint. She could do this without him. She had to.

He cast a look at her, but didn't take the bait. He simply grunted and tucked a stray swaddling blanket into the diaper bag, then put away his tablet, which he'd brought along to catch up on work of his own during a baby feeding.

A tap on the door stopped her before she could volley a lawyerly retort his way.

Royce called, "Come in."

Of course he did. He'd won the battle by default. And she knew she was acting prickly, but being with him was difficult and too easy all at the same time.

The door opened and a woman peeked around it,

her long blond hair swinging. “Excuse me for interrupting. I have those files you asked for.”

Right. The files. The main reason for coming here. Naomi smiled in gratitude at Glenna’s new assistant. “Thank you, Milla. Sorry to have slipped in while you were out for lunch. We’re so glad to have you working for the family company.” Then she turned to Royce, grateful to have the woman in the room as an extra barrier to protect her from the crackling emotions between them. “Have you had a chance to meet Milla Jones?”

Six

Her heart pounding, Milla studied Naomi and Royce, having seen the pair only from a distance at the hospital as they'd walked down the corridor with the two bassinets. She'd been careful not to be observed during her just-before-dawn flower deliveries. Although that hallway moment had been a near miss. She'd almost been spotted where she shouldn't have been and blown her whole cover as a new employee for Alaska Oil Barons, Inc. If one of them had remembered her from her job interview…

Perhaps she'd been reckless in indulging in that night to scope out the families. But the temptation had been irresistible to see them in a relaxed moment, unguarded.

Here in the office was different. They had on their business faces, with all the walls that entailed. She was taking a risk, but having an "in" here was too important. She had access to records that she wouldn't have elsewhere. Records that could provide answers. Justice.

Peace.

Milla extended her hand to Royce Miller, glad she'd taken the time to get a manicure to lessen the ragged look of her chewed nails. "Nice to meet you." She'd met Naomi at the interview stage, but not him. "I only just started officially today, although I shadowed my predecessor last week. I understand you've all been busy these past couple of weeks with those two adorable babies."

Royce Miller was a scientist of formidable reputation. She'd done her research on that score. But she'd been unprepared for the full effect of his appeal close up. He was tall and lean, his shoulders stretching the fabric of the simple cashmere sweater he wore over a T. Casual clothes, yes. But the fabric was rich, the tailoring custom. People like Royce and Naomi moved in a whole different world.

The towering guy had shutters in his eyes, a guarded, brooding aura. "Welcome, Ms. Jones."

"Thank you. It's been a wonderful, busy first day." She passed the file and disc to Naomi.

Milla couldn't help but notice Naomi wore embroidered leather boots without a care for the brutal Alaska weather, no doubt because she could afford to replace them at will. Her Italian leather handbag was the kind shopkeepers kept behind a locked counter. Milla thought she remembered it from last year's fashion magazines, not that she'd ever been able to afford anything from the pages.

Naomi took the data and slid it into her briefcase. "Royce has been a tremendous help to the company—and to me."

Gossip about Royce and Naomi had flowed through the break room at lunch earlier. There was even a betting pool over whether they would reunite. "I imagine twins are quite exhausting."

Naomi's tired face lightened with a smile. "And a blessing."

"Of course," Milla answered, curious, needing to get a solid read of the major players here, to effectively achieve her goal of sabotaging the merger. The six Steele offspring and four Mikkelsons would not be joining forces, not as long as she drew breath. "I don't have children of my own, but I can imagine."

Naomi waved to the crib tucked in the corner. "Would you like to see them?"

Milla stifled a wince. She didn't doubt her mission here, but she didn't want to think of innocents. That only complicated things. She preferred to keep her focus on the guilty. Ultimately, the most effective way to protect the innocent. "I wouldn't want to wake them."

No way around this.

Smiling, Naomi walked toward the crib. "We're about to put them in their car seats to leave, anyway."

Milla surrendered to the inevitable and crossed the room, her high heels sinking into the plush carpet. She peered into the crib, where the two infants slept side by side, their heads touching. "They both have a full head of dark hair." She clutched the side of the crib, clenching her hands to keep from reaching inside. From making a connection, its own sort of sabotage. "They're beautiful."

Even as Milla glanced at the sleeping babies, her throat went tight. To see this through, she needed to remain apart. Distant. She concentrated on the designer blankets instead of those sweet faces.

"Thank you." Naomi stepped closer, stopping beside her. "They look like my mother. In fact, Mary is named for her."

"That's a lovely tribute." Milla backed away, needing space and air to regain her conviction. "I should get to work, and I'm sure you're ready to head home. Feel free to call if you need anything while your assistant is on vacation."

Milla spun on her heels and left, closing the door after her, then sagging back against her desk. She'd done a lot of things she wasn't proud of over the years. Necessary, but choices that haunted her at times. She didn't regret the decision to start this path.

She just hadn't expected it would be so difficult to see it through.

* * *

Royce focused on the road ahead of him, needing a task, routine, control to keep him from being too aware of the woman next to him. He had to keep his head if he expected to make the most of his time with her and the twins. Easier said than done when Naomi had a way of making his go-to logic tough as hell to find.

He gripped the leather-trimmed steering wheel of his new SUV. Of course, this vehicle was nearly identical to his previous one, just a year newer. This version boasted the same attention to detail. The same precision engineering that he'd researched thoroughly the first time he'd purchased one. A methodical man, a scientist, Royce liked repeatable, predictable patterns. The uniformity of results gave him an anchor in an otherwise chaotic world.

And as he guided the new SUV around a tight mountainside curve with Naomi and her daughters in tow, he wanted something reliable.

No extra surprises. Royce had a general idea of how this model would handle in difficult terrain. Which was a good call, considering the snow-capped mountain they were winding around still had evidence of the mudslide from a storm a few weeks ago. The sludge-covered roads stirred a deep worry in his gut, momentarily flashing him back to the moment the twins were born. How that night had been everything but predictable.

It had required all his willpower to shut down

the gut-deep fear for Naomi and focus on keeping her calm while guiding the babies into the world.

Nightmares plagued him about all the things that could have gone wrong. The hell that would have haunted him if she or the babies hadn't made it.

Snowflakes melted as soon as they hit the heated windshield. Glancing quickly in the rearview mirror, he let out a sigh of relief. The road was theirs. No one in sight.

A strange sense of calm washed over him. Being in the car with the twins and Naomi felt so damn natural. Even more so since they'd taken a detour to get his Saint Bernard. Tessie rested in the far back, curled up on a quilt. They'd placed two baby blankets there as well, one from each of the girls so the dog would grow accustomed to their scent. She rested her big head on the seat, staring at the babies, sniffing the air, but unable to reach them because of her seat belt tether.

And sure, Royce found his attention drifting to Naomi more than he should, the creamy line of her jaw as she relaxed back in her seat. That easy smile she wore. Her hair flowing in deep waves.

Turning her gaze from the window, she checked on the sleeping girls behind them. Then called out soothing words of praise to Tessie before glancing at him.

"Royce, thanks again for helping today."

He kept his eyes firmly on the road, all too conscious of the precious cargo in the vehicle. "You've thanked me already."

"I couldn't have done it without you."

"I beg to differ." He shook his head as the road dipped around a cluster of pine trees. "You would have managed with your sister or a nanny."

"Maybe I could have." Sighing, she turned toward him, her forehead furrowed. "Are you regretting volunteering for this unconventional setup? Because if you are, I understand. I really can ask my family for help. Maybe you should go to your place for a while."

The thought of trusting the safety of her and the twins to someone else? No. He couldn't, and he didn't want to analyze the why of that. "You're not getting rid of me that easily."

"I wish I understood better why you're insisting on us spending time together. Maybe I'm just too brain tired, but this doesn't seem to be bringing closure."

He wished he had the answer to that. But he was sorting it out. Still, she clearly expected him to respond, so he opted for something that would buy him more time. "I thought these girls were going to be mine. I'm learning to say goodbye."

Exhaling hard, she sagged back in her seat. "I thought that might be the case, because of what happened with your ex-fiancée." Her throat moved with a hard swallow as she blinked fast. "I appreciate your honesty."

Hell, he hadn't meant to hurt her—again. Communication wasn't his forte, even more so when dealing with Naomi. In the past, he'd relied more on their intense physical connection. Although backtracking to repair their communication would only make things worse, since he didn't have a better answer on how to try.

Regardless, they were locked into seeing each other for the remaining year on his contract consulting for her family's oil company. A year of wanting her. A year of remembering what it had been like to have her in his arms, in his bed.

He winced.

The best course? Dig in for the next four weeks and hope they both found what they were looking for to put the past to rest.

Naomi couldn't believe she was back at the office again.

Her maternity leave was not turning out the way she'd planned. But with the merger in the works and the future of her family's business at stake, she had to balance it all. For the past ten days, she'd fallen into a rhythm of coming to the office for an hour a day to take care of business that needed addressing in person. The hour also gave her a break from the connection with Royce that she absolutely could not surrender to. She'd let him go for both of their sakes, and with him underfoot, she needed an excuse to break the spell her mind wanted to weave.

She unpacked her briefcase onto the desk, time being of the essence. The babies napped long enough in the afternoon that she could be away for a short period of time without hauling them from home. Royce swore he enjoyed the quiet time while the babies slept to accomplish work of his own.

She could see that her huge family was starting to wear on him, yet he wasn't budging. And she couldn't bring herself to boot him out. God, they were a messed up ex-couple.

Shaking off the distracting thoughts, she settled in front of the computer. Slipping into work mode, she embraced feeling in the zone. Her fingers flew at the speed of light across the keyboard as she plowed through the work in front of her, to be ready for her meeting with Chuck Mikkelson. Officially her stepbrother now, but also a force to be reckoned with in the Mikkelson empire. She couldn't afford to assume someone didn't have a hidden agenda just because they were family now and merging the companies.

Taking a deep breath, she pressed the button to buzz for Glenna's new assistant, Milla Jones.

Deep down, Naomi knew she needed to delegate. But admitting she needed help went against all she'd worked so hard to become. Still, exhaustion crept in. She buzzed again.

"Is there a problem?" A soft voice with a trace of a Canadian accent filtered through the sleek speaker.

Tucking a pen behind her ear, Naomi scanned the desk again. Nope. No sign of the much needed files. She let go an exasperated sigh. “I can’t seem to locate the files I need for my meeting with Chuck Mikkelson.”

“What files would those be?”

Removing the pen from behind her ear, Naomi leaned forward on Glenna’s desk. Dropping her head in her palm, she rubbed her temple, stress mounting. “The numbers Glenna and Broderick worked up on the improvements to the pipeline to North Dakota.”

“I have them right here on my desk. Give me two seconds.” The speaker went silent and moments later the door opened. Milla pulled a stack of files from under her arm. “They’re in here.”

“Oh, thank you.” Naomi reached for them, unable to help but notice how chic and put together the blonde looked, with perfect waves in her hair and not a wrinkle in her pencil skirt. “I was concerned I left some brain cells at the girls’ 3:00 a.m. feeding.”

Naomi resisted the urge to smooth a hand over her leggings, one of the few things that fit, along with one of Royce’s cotton button-downs she’d grabbed off the back of a chair. She’d been running late, so hurriedly threw on a chunky necklace and leather boots. She needed to go shopping, but time was limited these days.

“I’m in awe you’re here.” The assistant tapped the two files. “I’ve emailed copies, as well.”

“You’re efficient. I appreciate your help.”

Milla tipped her head to the side, surveying the office with great intensity before shrugging on her way out. "Just learning my way around, getting to know all the people."

The door clicked closed, leaving Naomi alone again. The hair on the nape of her neck prickled. Something about the new assistant felt…off. Something she couldn't quite articulate or grasp, but the same spidery sense that sometimes tingled during court cases.

Shaking her head, she decided it must be the lack of sleep playing with her instincts. She should be digging into the files rather than letting her mind wander.

Just as she reached for them, a tall, ruggedly handsome man with sandy brown hair walked into her office without being announced. Chuck, her once rival turned stepbrother. She and her family hadn't seen much of Chuck lately, since he and his wife had been having marital troubles. During Jack Steele's recovery from surgery, they'd all been so overwhelmed, they'd had to recruit the younger Mikkelson brother—Trystan—to be the face of the blending companies at a major fund-raiser. It had required one helluva media and mouth makeover to get the volatile, outspoken, rugged rancher camera ready.

Of course, Trystan's attraction to the media consultant had provided a hefty motivation to succeed. Now they were engaged and expected a baby.

Chuck was back at the helm now, though. And early for this meeting, to boot. A sinking feeling tightened her chest. She hadn't even had the opportunity to crack open the paperwork and skim. Too late now, however. She would have to wing it.

Naomi stepped from behind the desk. "So, hello...*stepbrother*. How crazy is that?"

"Completely." He set his briefcase on the coffee table between the two sofas, looking professional as always, but also like he had the weight of the world on his shoulders. "I think it's going to take us all a while to get used to this unlikely blended family. Everyone sends their best on the babies' safe arrival."

"Blessings doubled and troubles shared. Thank you for all the flowers and the hospital visit." Office talk could wait for a moment. She'd deposed enough witnesses to know that things went smoother when they were at ease. She went to the wet bar and tapped the carafe. "Coffee?"

"Yes, thank you," he said. "Although I'm not so sure I've done my share with helping."

"Trystan and his image consultant pulled off a top-notch coup at the Wilderness Preservation fundraiser."

"Surprised us all, quite frankly. I knew he could do it, but he exceeded expectations."

Trystan had a reputation for being brusque and antisocial. He'd been adopted by the Mikkelson family—a cousin with a rocky start in life.

"Together, we'll all make this happen. Thank you for being flexible about the time today. I, um, realize your plate's full. I'm sorry about the trouble you and Shana have been having…" Naomi paused, setting aside the carafe. "I hope that was okay to say. I didn't mean to get too personal."

"Everyone knows we've been struggling and how much time I've had to take off work." He took the china cup without adding cream or sugar.

She certainly understood the hardships a rocky relationship brought to every other aspect of life.

"If there's something I can do to help, let me know. Even if you just need a sympathetic ear." She poured herself a glass of sparkling water and sat on one of the sofas, bright light pouring in the huge wall of windows beside them.

"Unless you can change the past, I'm afraid not." Sitting across from her, he blew into his coffee before taking a hefty swallow.

"I heard she had a difficult time with her father." Vague details, but enough to make Naomi so grateful for her own steady dad. Jack Steele had been a rock for his children, even when suffering from a deep grief over losing his wife and one of his kids.

"That's putting it mildly." Chuck stared down into his cup of java. "I'm sure you'll hear eventually, now that our families are so tangled up. When Shana was a teenager, she found out that her 'hero' dad was a fraud. He wasn't some undercover detective. He was a rent-a-cop who had a second family tucked away a couple of counties over."

"Ohmigod, that's…awful." She'd heard about Shana's father walking out on his family, but not a whisper about this level of betrayal. And for some reason this was prevalent in Chuck's mind right now. Naomi stayed silent, letting him decide if he wanted to tell more or shift to work.

"Cheating is bad enough, but he deliberately posed as husband-and-wife with the other woman. Poured out his inheritance on her and her children at the expense of his own—not to mention the time he chose to be away from his own kids."

"Shana must have been crushed. I can't imagine what kind of person would do that to his own child."

Chuck forked his hand through his hair, a trace of anger sparking in his eyes. "A raging narcissist who's only interested in looking good in front of others, who feeds off emotions. It's all about manipulating life to what serves him best. That has made it difficult for Shana to trust."

"Her father's still alive?" Naomi rubbed her arms, goose bumps rising. She couldn't imagine hurting her children that way.

"He lives down in San Diego with his new wife, in a house on the beach that was bought with all the money he funneled into her name." Chuck held up a hand. "I'm sorry for unloading all of this on you. It's just fresh on my mind, since we heard from the guy yesterday."

The legal eagle part of her wanted to find a way to nail the guy, to get justice for Shana. "Um, what stops you from—"

"Killing him for crushing my wife?" he asked

tightly. "For destroying her mother? For being the lowest form of scum on the earth?" His jaw went tight. "I get by knowing that karma will nail him. Knowing he lost amazing people in his life and he's now with a person who thought nothing of living a lie and destroying a family." Shrugging, he smiled. "And I don't want to go to jail."

She laughed softly. "There is that."

"Yeah, seriously, though, Shana says attention is what he craves, so she ignores him. He pops his head up for air every now and again to try to stir things up."

"I'm so sorry."

"I'm sorry he hurt my wife, that he has made it so difficult for her to trust. She deserves good things in life." Chuck reached for his china cup on the coffee table.

"Trust..." Naomi shook her head. "I wrestle with that and I haven't faced near what she did. I know my family loves me."

"You lost your mother and sister. You've battled cancer. You've had your fair share of kicks from life. It's not a game of whose pain is worse. Pain is pain." He cricked his neck from side to side, his face going neutral, as if he'd placed all that anger into a box and sealed it shut. "We should get to work."

"Of course, you're right. I'm sorry for prying."

He waved dismissively. "You weren't. You're just good at asking questions and listening." His eyes narrowed wryly. "I imagine it comes with your job."

"I'm no expert at relationships. I think in listening to how other people sort through things, I'm trying to find answers for my own life." She nudged the files on the coffee table toward him. "So, back to work. I haven't had a chance to look over these numbers from Glenna and Broderick. How about you tell me your take on things before I do."

Royce's ecological innovations put every other version of oil production to shame. They could not and would not risk the wilderness they loved so much. Now there was the teeny-tiny matter of making Royce's design financially feasible.

Chuck reached for his briefcase. "There's no way around it. The numbers just don't work."

Finally, he had some much needed solitude to lose himself in business, and yet he was still tense as hell.

Royce drummed his fingers next to his computer on the teak desk, his dog napping at his feet. He'd taken time off, but his work was about more than clocking in hours for a paycheck. His occupation as a research scientist was a calling for him, a way of life to protect the future for children like Anna and Mary.

Which meant working with the Steele-Mikkelsons at Alaska Oil Barons, Inc. was his best bet for making his theories come to life. Yet another reason he had to figure out this relationship with Naomi, as they were tied together through the company. There was no avoiding each other if things went south between them again. He wasn't budging from his plan to stay until her father returned for the party that would welcome him and Jeannie.

Royce glanced at his watch and saw Naomi should be arriving home any minute now. She'd texted him when she left the office. He'd had the chef send up supper so he and Naomi could eat in her suite.

Time to stretch his legs. Which was really just an excuse to check on the girls. Sure, he had the video baby monitor hooked up, which he frequently glanced at, but seeing them with his own two eyes soothed him. Tessie stood, then loped alongside him, her tail wagging. She'd taken well to the little ones, often alerting to their coos and squawks an instant prior to the monitor picking up the sounds. Luckily, the Steeles were open to dogs, one thing he had in common with them. Tessie enjoyed romping in the snow with Glenna and Broderick's husky.

Royce looked into the bassinet, relieved that they still slept. Didn't even stir. God, they were cute, and fast wrapping him around their tiny little fingers. He rubbed the back of his neck and turned away.

A grumble in his stomach led him to the kitchen, where the chef had left a mouthwatering caribou stew, and rhubarb crisp for dessert. As he lifted the lid on the pot to stir the stew, he heard the elevator whirring closer. The doors slid open and Naomi strode inside her L-shaped corner suite.

Damn, she was gorgeous, with her legs showcased in leggings and leather boots. She was wearing one of his shirts, along with a bulky jewel-toned necklace… His mouth went dry and he reminded himself he had to stay away from her not just for physical reasons, but also for their very sanity.

He shook off thoughts he wasn't close to having answers for.

"Welcome back." He tossed a hand towel over his shoulder. "How did your meeting go?"

"Busy." She set aside her briefcase, a strand of hair slipping free from her topknot. "Let's talk about yours. How are the babies? I hope they didn't run you ragged."

"The girls napped. Then your sister came up. Some of the Mikkelsons were with her—don't ask me which ones—and they took the twins downstairs." A reminder of how soon she would realize she didn't need him. And then what? Could he just walk away? Was closure possible? "There were plenty of capable hands to hold and feed the babies."

"The wonders of a big family," she muttered, stretching her arms, the shirt pulling taught against her breasts.

"You have a pack, for sure." He stifled a wince at the mention of her large family. The last thing he wanted was to set her defenses up, but damn, his brain was on stun from taking in her curves.

"What did you all talk about?" She peeked into the pot on the stove, breathing in the aroma with a blissful expression. When she stirred it with a spoon and tasted it, her sexy moan almost drove him to his knees.

"I went to the study." He hauled his attention away and pulled a large bottled water from the stainless steel refrigerator. "Work."

"Right, of course. I'm being selfish. I know how important your research is to you."

Something shifted in her deep brown eyes that he couldn't quite place. But then his brain wasn't chugging on all cylinders with his body aching to be near her.

"It is," he said, pouring water into two cut crystal glasses. "But for this phase, I'm through with the bulk of the heavy lifting. It's about implementation now."

She turned her back to pull bowls from the cabinet, her focus on picking at the food and setting the table, his on the movement of her mouth as she licked her fingers. He recalled the day they'd first met, when they'd been alone in that tiny glass igloo-style retreat outside Anchorage. The way her eyes had roamed over him. He wanted that attention now.

She turned from the table, facing him. "And your next consulting project?"

"Does this mean I'm fired?" He offered it as a joke, but the answer mattered more than he cared to admit. He couldn't delude himself. He wasn't ready to leave.

She glanced at him, eyes wide. "No, of course

not. Just making conversation. Wondering about your future."

"I have files full of ideas. I'm almost considering taking some long-term time off after this project. Recharge the brain." Get over the hellish fallout from having walked away from her for good. "That's when the best inventions happen. Trust me, though, my entire focus is on this project. It's important to me."

She chewed her bottom lip, concern for him so evident in her eyes that it reached into him, drew him closer. And even though he knew touching her couldn't lead anywhere right now, he stroked her face…

And covered her mouth with his.

Seven

Naomi gripped Royce's shoulders, her fingers digging into the hard planes.

To push him away?

Or to bring him closer?

No choice at all. A simple decision. The draw to share this moment with him was too strong.

Her hands slid around his shoulders and up into his hair, then she leaned into him, soaking up the familiar feel of him. Starved for him after so long apart. His strong arms banded around her waist, his palms roving over her back.

She'd missed the focus on *her* as a woman. Need returned with a vengeance. To indulge. To know she was an indulgence to him.

A low growl rumbled through his chest, vibrating against her. She sighed, threading her fingers through his hair.

He stroked her shoulders, then down her arms as he arched away. He cupped the back of her head and guided it to rest against his chest. "Naomi, I shouldn't have done that."

She wasn't sure if she appreciated him stopping or not. But she couldn't deny every second of that kiss had been delicious. Welcome.

"We can't pretend the past doesn't exist." She searched for words to ease the awkwardness—and the pain of lost dreams. Her fingers moved against the crisp cotton of his shirt. "We were drawn to each other for a reason back then. Even going our separate ways doesn't erase that initial pull or what we almost had."

"How about we agree we're not pretending anymore, but we also shelve this discussion for now? It's been a long day."

She pulled away, more stung by his avoiding the discussion than she wanted to admit. He was so very obviously escaping.

Her pride hurt too much, though, to challenge him on that. So she embraced the exhaustion excuse. "Of course. You're right." She backed away from him. "I could use a catnap before the girls wake up. And please don't offer to watch them for me. Go. Take some time for yourself."

He studied her for five heartbeats before nodding

slowly. "I'm going to pick up some things from my place and grab supper out. Call me if you need me before the girls settle in for the night."

Snagging his coat from the back of the sofa on his way to the elevator, he walked away without another word. Leaving her alone with the girls and her thoughts.

Her mind churned with memories of that kiss, the rasp of his fingers on her skin, the taste of him. She'd missed his touch, his kisses.

She'd missed *him.*

Goose bumps prickled as she rubbed her arms. The girls were sleeping, and she was alone. She should be doing something other than wandering around the living room in circles. At the very least, she should shower and sleep, two things in short supply for her these days.

A half hour later, she slid under the covers with a hefty sigh. The babies snoozed on in their nursery and she'd placed the monitor beside her bed, even though her door was open as well as theirs.

As sleep swept over her, her languid thoughts drifted back to Royce's kiss, to so many other kisses. Their attraction had been undeniable from the moment she'd met him, trapped together in an all-glass igloo-style cabin during a blizzard… That chemistry had drawn them into bed so quickly, so very memorably. The desire to leave the heartache behind fell away as the dream drew her under…

Royce's mouth and hands set her body on fire,

and as much as part of her shouted that this was happening too fast, she also knew her days for having a no-strings fling were numbered. Casual would take on a different meaning once she gave birth. On a practical level, having a wild, torrid affair with him right now, in this bed made complete sense.

Royce angled back to look into her eyes, stroking her hair with a long sweep of his hands. "Are you sure this is what you want?"

"Are you kidding me? I very much want you."

He eyed her with a gaze that drank her in, launching another wave of excitement through her veins. Anticipation swirled through her until her face heated with a flush. He reached into the bedside table and pulled out an unopened box of condoms.

Morning sunshine pushed through the snow on the glass roof, dappling them with light as she tugged at his shirt and sweatpants. His skin was impossibly warm, the hard muscles shifting under her touch while she skimmed away his clothes. The expanse of his muscled chest sprinkled with hair wasn't that of a sedentary man. The sinewy planes of him spoke of activity, of a love of the outdoors.

She wanted to feel him, all of him, against her. Inside her. She'd never been so hot, so hungry, for any man. She reveled in the graze of his fingers as he bunched and swept aside her silk thermal shirt, sliding around the strap of the simple cotton bra she'd never planned on anyone else seeing. His avid gaze practically sizzled the fabric away, her breasts beading to aching points by the time he freed her. She shivered as he scraped down the thermal underwear, until at last they were skin to skin.

The warmth of him, pressing flesh to flesh as he kissed her, ramped up her need higher, hotter. He skimmed his mouth to the curve of her neck and she caught a glimpse of the heat in his eyes as he stroked her with his gaze, as tangible as his hands caressing her breasts. Then lower, kissing the inside of her thigh before moving to the core of her. Circling, plucking. Teasing a tingling flame higher and hotter until her own hands clenched into fists.

"You're absolutely...gorgeous. But you have to already know that."

His intuitive touch made her feel carefree. They were just man and woman, caught up in a feverish attraction. She'd had no idea how powerful that could be.

"You're making me blush."

Royce planted slow, deliberate kisses on her collarbone. "That sounds like an invitation to make you blush all over."

Oh. My.

Breath seemed impossible as he pressed against her. Still, somehow she managed to whisper, "As long as turnabout is fair play."

"Yes, ma'am." His confident chuckle heated her flesh and he angled up to graze his mouth along her ear, her jaw.

"And by the way?"

"Yeah?"

"You're too chatty." She nipped his bottom lip.

His slow, sexy smile gave her an instant's warning before his mouth closed over her breast, one then the other, until the tingles gathered force within her to a tight urgency.

She grabbed for the box of condoms and wrenched it open, fumbling to tear into a packet. He reached for her hand, but she nudged him aside. Wanting. Needing to explore him. She sheathed him and his groan of pleasure brought an answering groan from her.

"Naomi, there are so many more ways I want to touch you, to—"

She pressed a finger to his lips. "And you can. We will. Right now, though..."

She didn't have to finish the thought. He slid inside her, filling her as her legs glided up and around his hips, her ankles locking. In sync, they moved. She didn't know how to explain the strength of sensations already swelling inside her, the way his caresses ignited her, knew her so instinctively. Being with him was insane and somehow so damn right all at the same time...

Pacing in the dark nursery, Royce shushed the fussy baby in his arms, Anchorage's skyline twinkling in the distance. "Your mama's tired, and she's finally not restless. Let's keep it quiet." He kept walking the floor, glad he'd thought to turn off the nursery monitor and close Naomi's bedroom door when he'd returned. "Shall I recite the periodic table to you? I could even sing it."

The tiny face scrunched up, feet pumping.

"Good choice. My voice is nails on a chalkboard. So if you're not into the periodic table, I could shuffle to Newton's Laws of Motion, Hubble's Law of Cosmic Expansion, Universal Law of Gravitation, Archimedes's Buoyancy Principle? Surely I must be boring you to sleep."

Mary blinked again, wide-awake. Yes, Mary. He might not be able to tell one Mikkelson from another, but he could tell the difference between Mary and Anna by the way their eyebrows grew. Even their cries were a little different. The infant shoved a fist into her mouth and sucked, watching him.

He welcomed this time alone to get his thoughts together after that combustible kiss with Naomi. And he couldn't avoid the truth—that he'd wanted to keep on kissing her. Having her in his arms again had been incredible.

Leaving after the gala was going to be tougher than he'd bargained on. Work with the pipeline modifications would ramp up for him, but the evenings would be lonely. Gaining closure and getting her out of his mind wasn't panning out as he'd expected.

Throughout the last few weeks, Royce had attempted to bury the surprise of how naturally and easily he fitted into their routine. But alone with the babies, late at night with nothing but a twinkling city skyline, the reality of how right it felt became undeniable. It was about more than fitting into a routine. It was about the joy of a daily connection.

Mary squawked again and he jostled her lightly, whispering, "If you were older I would let you play with the abacus." His chest went tight, that fear of a future without Naomi creeping back in. "I hope I get to see that one day, kiddo. I can't make any promises, though, because it's up to your mama how that plays out."

He thought of Naomi sleeping just a door away, that glimpse of her burned into his brain. How she sprawled blissfully under the comforter, her hair splayed out on the pillow. Not too many months ago, he would have had the right to turn his face into those silky strands. Their relationship had had a combustible start and an equally explosive ending. He couldn't envision them finding a peaceful friendship. They were an all-or-nothing kind of couple.

Could she have had a point? That he was pursuing her only because he wanted a replacement family? He hated to think that of himself. And damn it, he knew his attraction to Naomi was real. Her intelligence and take-no-prisoners attitude made her irresistible.

But he also knew he wasn't one to deal with emotions. He avoided those memories at all costs. Maybe the babies were bringing the whole of his past out again.

But two things were evident. He couldn't fix what

was wrong between him and Naomi, and he loved the babies, had since before they were born. He was their father in all the ways that mattered, and he was going to bring the fight to them, not let go.

He had a few more weeks to figure this out. Maybe, with time, he and Naomi would find that their connection, their shared interest at work, and yes, raising these two babies together, was more than enough to bind them together.

Or was that just wishful thinking?

The L-shaped loft could not contain Naomi's racing mind. She poked at her eggs with a fork tip, chasing them around the dish—an heirloom from her grandmother—trying to bring her world, heart and mind into balance. Trying to channel the scales of Justice. But rather than needing the scales to sort out a complex legal problem, Naomi needed them to settle the affairs of her heart.

Royce sat across from her in sweats and an MIT T-shirt that stretched across his muscular chest. Sitting here with him was too intimate, with the memory of that kiss and the resulting dream smoking through her mind.

She averted her eyes, which didn't help at all when her gaze landed on the suitcase he'd been living out of since she and the girls got home from the hospital. Now, an empty suitcase. While she'd napped, he'd unpacked everything and stowed his gear in the extra closet and shelves in her bedroom.

Just as he had when they'd lived here together, alternating between her place and his until they came up with a more permanent plan. Something that never happened.

"Royce, you have to know it's presumptuous of you to move in here."

He glanced at her, raising one eyebrow, but staying silent.

Damn, but he was arrogant. And hot.

"Tall, dark and brooding isn't going to work on me. We need to set some ground rules if we're going to spend this time together."

And damn it, she realized she'd just conceded he was staying. Apparently tall, dark and brooding did work.

"Royce..."

"Yes?" His voice rumbled in the space between them, luring her.

"Just, um, no more kissing." She started to say more about the presumption of his virtual move-in, but that seemed silly when she was depending on him so much. "I'm taking the girls today and I insist you have the day for yourself."

"What if I say no?"

She bit back the urge to snap, and reached for the decaf coffee. Surely it was the lack of caffeine while still nursing the babies that was making her cranky. "I *will* call you crazy if you turn down the time. Seriously, I'm spending the day with Chuck's wife, Shana. We're putting our heads together for the welcome home party."

He stared at her with narrowed eyes, as if weighing her words for an ulterior motive in sending him off. The downside to having been a couple. He knew her well.

Finally, he turned his attention to spreading berry jam on a thick slice of toast. "She's a good daughter-in-law to do that for Jeannie."

"They all appear to be close. There aren't as many Mikkelsons as there are Steeles, but they're working hard to pull equal hours." She tapped her fingers on the coffee mug.

"You sound…skeptical." Tearing off an edge of toast, he popped it into his mouth, then chewed thoughtfully.

His eyes met hers in that direct way of his that made her feel she had his full and undivided attention. A heady sensation out of bed as well as in. His tousled bed head made her fingers ache to smooth through the strands of hair, to touch him.

She looked at him over her cup of decaf java. "It's hard to trust them after so many years being mortal enemies. I cut my teeth on tales of how Mikkelsons ate kids for dinner."

"I can't envision your dad saying that to his children." Royce bit into the toast, his eyes skating to the nursery.

Her heart tugged at the thought of how much it would hurt him to tell the girls goodbye. But what was she supposed to do? "My brother said so. He seemed wise and ancient then. Sounds silly now, but the foundation for distrust was laid."

Royce set down the last bite of his toast slowly, deliberately. "Do you still question the Mikkelsons' ethics?"

His voice was steady, but genuine concern trickled through.

The very idea made her gut clench, especially with Royce's research on the line…

Could Chuck have an ulterior motive in stating the financials didn't work? But the numbers were the numbers. Unless he'd found a way to turn investors.

She hated having to think this way. But years as a corporate lawyer meant she *had* to.

She drew a breath. "I wouldn't go that far without proof. More like I question their loyalty, because I know my family will always come first for me. Why wouldn't they feel the same?"

"You seemed to have resolved that before."

"It was easier to try to believe all would be well in the beginning. And then Dad was in the horse riding accident and business affairs were the last thing on our minds. Now, when it's getting to crunch time with the final stages of the merger…it's just tougher." Naomi's nerves churned again. Protecting the family, her family, informed every decision she'd ever made. With two daughters of her own to consider, her resolve doubled.

"What choices do you have?" Royce leaned

forward, palms splayed. She could reach out and touch him, like old times. Naomi wanted to feel the strength and warmth of the scientist's fingertips. But that would only make things even more complicated. Blurry as a snowstorm. Perhaps just as dangerous, too.

Instead, she gripped her decaf tighter. "Not many. I'm keeping my eyes open, checking and double-checking documents..."

Royce nodded, his dark eyes registering more and more. "The reason you keep insisting on working."

"Yes." Talking to him was such an easy habit to fall into again. Only three weeks and she was already weakening. "And I'm watching the other side."

"You think Shana may not be as guarded."

It had crossed her mind. God, he read her so well. "Either way, we have to plan the party. We're related by in-law something. It's worth talking to her."

"All right, then." Palms on the table, he stood, pausing, then nodding. "I'll make a plate for myself and gratefully hide out in the study to work. Text if you need me."

He skimmed a hand across her shoulder, the casual touch intimate in its own way. Her breath hitched and she couldn't keep from watching how he moved, loading up with breakfast, his strides to the elevator even, heavy. She wanted to call him back, to share breakfast, to hold his hand and even flirt as if they didn't have a past. As if they'd just met.

The elevator doors slid open, and Royce gestured

for Shana to enter the suite before he disappeared from view.

Shana clutched a three-ring binder and a tablet, walking closer. "I can come back later if I was interrupting..."

"No, please," Naomi said, smoothing her loose tunic and leggings. "Royce has work to do. The girls are asleep. The timing is perfect. Join me for some breakfast while we go over the plans?"

Shana half turned, the bell sleeves of her dress swishing. "Sure, if you're absolutely certain you wouldn't just rather relax with—"

Sighing, Naomi rolled her eyes. "Is it that obvious to everyone how..."

"Confused you're feeling?" Shana sat at the table, setting the binder and tablet aside. "Not to everyone. I was a successful detective for a reason." She reached for the orange juice, the morning sun hitting her thick, long hair as she leaned forward.

Shana hadn't needed to scrape her locks into a messy bun this morning.

"I was so sure when I broke things off with him it was the right thing to do." Naomi touched her own topknot, which was full of tangles from sleeping with her hair wet. Or moving restlessly in the night because of her dreams. "I know I should let him go, but it doesn't feel right anymore. Part of me wants a second chance."

Though she still needed to determine Chuck's and his family's motives businesswise, Naomi found herself at ease with Shana on this subject, at least. Walls and pretenses were evaporating. The woman was becoming more than just a step-in-law. She was becoming a friend.

"That's not a question I can answer for you." Shana eyed her over the glass of juice.

"You're married. You've worked through hard times." Naomi wondered if she'd overstepped, but Shana and Chuck's marital troubles hadn't been a secret.

"I wouldn't say we've worked through them." The leggy blonde swept a lock of hair off her forehead before settling into the chair. "More like we've worked on them."

"I'm sorry. I didn't mean to pry." So much for Naomi's plan to find out more about the Mikkelson family business.

Laughing, Shana waved aside her concern. "We're family now, in a roundabout way. Step-in-laws."

Naomi welcomed the release of a laugh after the tension of the morning with Royce. "I was just thinking the same thing. I look forward to getting to know everyone better."

"Do you trust him?"

Startled at the question, Naomi looked up sharply. Shana couldn't have read her mind about Chuck and the other Mikkelsons, could she?

Oh… Realization dawned. Shana meant did Naomi trust Royce. "Yes, I do."

And damn, but that took the wind right out of her sails. She didn't trust life to be kind to her, or to last. But the people in her world? They hadn't done anything like Shana's father had to her.

Naomi thought back to all Chuck had shared about his wife's past. The pain in Shana's eyes was tangible. Naomi squeezed her hand and an understanding passed between them, a sense that Shana could tell Naomi knew about the woman's father somehow.

Shana squeezed back. "A good, honest man that you can truly trust is worth giving a second chance."

The truth resonated. The stakes were so high with Naomi's children. Royce was digging in deep to make his mark with the company for years to come—although he didn't know about Chuck's numbers.

If he stayed with the company long term and Naomi and he crossed paths, this could make their relationship all the more tense. As if things weren't difficult enough to sift through.

Would Royce blame her for the failed number crunch?

Did *he* trust *her*?

Her heart hammered in her chest, the sound so loud it filled her ears. She still wanted him in spite of their problems and all the unresolved questions.

One way or another, she had to use these next

weeks together before the gala to find out how much of a chance she could afford to give him, because she feared another breakup would destroy them both.

Eight

Milla had breached the inner circle.

Well, at least superficially.

She'd been invited to a movie viewing in the plush screening room at the Mikkelson compound. Only a select few employees had been invited. She wasn't sure what had landed her on the list, but here she was.

Sconces on the wall reflected light in the shape of hourglasses. Subdued. Understated. And yet Milla recognized the luxury of the Mikkelsons' home theater.

No amount of low lighting could camouflage or downplay the rows of plush leather reclining seats that had built-in massage options. Never mind the grand hallway she'd walked through to arrive at the media room. The rich scent of mahogany paneling filled the air.

What must it be like to live here? Milla wondered, swirling the pinot noir in her glass.

She took a moment to appreciate her ability to move so seamlessly into this family's world. An infiltration James Bond would be proud of. Her success tonight was as tangible as the heavy plate of hors d'oeuvres she clutched in her due-for-a-manicure fingers.

As she noticed the flaking polish, she clenched her free hand into a fist, hiding her nails. Somehow fearing that the ragged edges of her hard-fought veneer would reveal her intentions to the whole room.

Milla shoved the thought down with a swig of wine. She needed this opportunity to get to know the key players better, in a more informal setting.

Leaning against the maroon wall, she surveyed the media room. Tried to take it all in. Note the family dynamics in this relaxed space. She smiled at two employees from the office who passed her to take seats in the front row.

Chuck and Shana Mikkelson sat side by side without touching. Something like ice seemed to settle in the space between them. The contrast was stark, given how Broderick's arm was around Glenna as his wife leaned her head on his shoulder.

Younger siblings, Aiden Steele and Alayna Mikkelson, whispered and laughed in the corner. Likely teenage stuff such as social media gossip, given their death grips on their devices.

Half a dozen other employees sprinkled throughout were eating gourmet popcorn and sipping cocktails.

And in the back, Delaney Steele and Birch Montoya. Why did everyone else buy their enemies act? Sure, they were on opposite sides of the environmental spectrum, but clearly, they were having a secret affair. The tension between them was so combustible Milla wouldn't have been surprised to see it light up the dark screening room.

They were all so wrapped up in their own worlds, their smaller circles that kept them from seeing outside to the larger picture.

She had to see it all. To absorb every morsel of information she could glean. Because someone here had betrayed her adoptive family in Canada. She owed her family everything—and that included seeing justice served.

Milla stacked her plate on a side table with the others, then moved toward the middle of a row. Settling into a seat there, she lifted her wineglass, hoping to seem as nonchalant as possible as she discreetly tuned into nearby, whispered conversations taking place before *Cyber Ghost* started.

Yet another mark of wealth she could not fully understand. The Mikkelsons were able to debut the film here—an exclusive showing of a feature simultaneously debuting in theaters tomorrow.

Aiden passed to take his seat, his popcorn box right at nose level so she couldn't miss the scent. From the aroma, it seemed a mixture of cheddar and…maple. Yes. Maple syrup.

Images of her adoptive family flooded her. Of warm breakfasts in a tiny, sterile room. Pancakes… The memories threatened to consume her. They might have succeeded, too, if not for the tall presence of Conrad Steele settling into a seat beside her.

Suddenly, she became hyperaware of the here and now.

Conrad was making the rounds in place of his older brother, Jack, who was still on his extended honeymoon. Conrad smiled, his blue-gray eyes searching hers as if he was trying to understand some essential truth about her in the minutes before the screening began.

He cleared his throat, leaning toward her, his elbows resting on his jeans-clad thighs. In a low voice that made her think of wind blowing through brush, he asked, "How are you liking working for the company? Is everybody treating you well?"

Milla tightened her grip on the stem of her leaded crystal glass. "Everyone's been very welcoming. Thank you for asking."

"It's a time of change," he said, leaning back in the chair, leather creaking, "which makes it all the tougher as a newcomer on staff."

Conrad lazily scratched his head, that smile still playing on his lips, crinkling the skin beside his eyes.

"Others are new, too." And she could get lost in the sea of new faces. Especially if she didn't make waves.

"I can see how that would offer more opportunities for friendships."

"Of course." Was he hitting on her? Sure, he was cute in a middle-aged kind of way. But still. Eww.

"Sage Hammond is about your age. She's good people. Reach out to her if you need anything."

Milla relaxed in the theater seat, relieved that she wouldn't have to rebuff a major Steele player. Yes, Conrad had his own corporate interests, but he was still the younger brother of Jack Steele and a significant stockholder in his own right. He'd even assisted Jack on occasion before the younger Steeles were old enough to help their father in the company.

In spite of his easygoing manner, Conrad Steele was not to be dismissed lightly.

The older man eyed his drained snifter. "Hmm, my drink's empty. Good to talk to you, and again, welcome."

Milla studied him as he walked away, wondering what secrets were hidden in his brain. He played the part so well, being half in, half out of this world. Like he was playing the odds, so he had a stake in a winning side either way.

How deep did his secret agendas go? And was anyone else in his family involved?

* * *

As the sun refracted on the fresh snow, Royce inhaled the cold air and awakened his insides with the bracing Alaskan atmosphere. The cool morning breeze raked across his cheeks as he sauntered forward. Everything felt crisper with Naomi around, sending his senses into hyperdrive.

She walked nearby as he pulled the babies in a stroller-style sleigh. Tessie bounded in the snow ahead, kicking up mini flurries.

It should have been a contented, peaceful kind of outing with Naomi. But the frustrated attraction between them sizzled so tangibly he wouldn't be surprised if the icicles started melting off the trees.

Cricking his neck from side to side, he tamped down the passion flaring to life inside him—or at least he tried to. The walk would be over soon. His willpower wouldn't have to be tested too long. Sunshine was brief in the winter. The baby sleigh made clean slices through the drifts as they walked alongside the bay. Having Naomi and the girls with him made the time bittersweet. He wanted to stretch out this outing—having her all to himself—as long as possible.

Restraint be damned.

He turned his head toward her, and her gaze collided with his. Some of his desire must have shown in his face because her pupils widened with awareness. She bit her bottom lip, then released it slowly.

With a brief shake of her head, she backed away.

The answering heat in her eyes was disguised with something else.

She'd put a wall between them. A wary one.

Naomi reached down, balling up snow in her gloved palm. Brunette hair fell, long and lovely, on her chest as she turned to him. An overbright smile played on pink lips that matched the pink in her cheeks. God, he wanted to kiss her mouth, stroke her face.

She packed the snowball between her gloved hands. "It's wonderful to be out here. I feel like I've been inside forever. Thank you for suggesting this."

Wind whipped, gusting her turquoise-and-feather earrings across her face. Ethereal and eclectic, Naomi floored him. Always. A life with her could never be boring. Royce swallowed hard.

"Wish I could claim unselfish motives in suggesting the walk. I'm enjoying the solitude." As if that were the only selfish motivation at play. He wanted time alone with her, away from all her relatives. His gaze raked over her again.

"Are we encroaching on your solitude?" She let the snowball fall from her hand. Her cautious question cut through him deeper than the wind. Time to shift away from controversial topics if he wanted a chance at another kiss. Thank goodness the twins were cooperating by sleeping in the sleigh.

"Not at all. This is what I wanted." The walk, the time with Naomi and the girls, with Tessie bounding through the snow.

"What you wanted for yourself was good for me, too. And the girls. There's nothing selfish about that." She held back a low hanging branch for Royce so he could pass through with the sleigh. A whiff of her perfume carried on the crisp breeze.

The brightness of the sun reflected in her eyes, distracting. Too much so. He nodded with a non-committal grunt.

"What's that supposed to mean?"

"Nothing." His boots crunched in the snow.

"I know you better than that." She tucked her hand in the crook of his arm, her eyes twinkling knowingly.

The muscles in his arm twitched in response to her touch. "Only trying to figure out how I could think that your love of the outdoors was enough to bind us. Well, that and an off-the-charts sex life."

There it was.

That awkward, weighted silence settled again in the air between them. A silence he felt in his chest and bones. A silence as cool as the northern wind sweeping across them.

He sighed hard, pressing on. Eyes catching on the horizon, where horses and riders gathered. The Mikkelsons and Steeles were making the most of the weekend. So much for solitude. One horse and rider descended in a headlong gallop. Royce couldn't help but watch the way the hooves of the horse seemed to glide across the snow like butter. Naomi let out a pained laugh. “Would you rather be riding? You don’t have to stay glued to my side.”

“This is where I want to be.” He paused for a moment, looking back at the twin girls in their orange snowsuits. Flicking his gaze back to the riders, he played with the lead in his hand before pulling on the sleigh again. There was much about this place to enjoy. “Although it would be nice if the twins were old enough to ride. With their genetics, I’m sure they’ll be in the saddle soon.”

“Lots of firsts to dream of for them. And individual pursuits, too. I want them to find their own favorites.”

Firsts he would miss out on. The hole in his heart felt wider than ever. “You’re already a great mom.” The wind picked up off the bay. Concerned for the twins, he steered them toward the boathouse.

“I appreciate that, but it’s still scarier than I expected.”

Royce locked his eyes forward. He wanted to make sure he’d be there for her. Provide support to her by helping with the girls. “You’ve taken on a lot in a short time.”

“I have an incredible amount of support and financial security.”

“That doesn’t automatically make life simple.” As they reached the boathouse, he gestured toward the door and shot her a questioning look.

She nodded, pushing it open, so he could slide the sleigh inside. He did so carefully, without waking the girls. "Well, all the support will help in the future," Naomi said.

"You can always call on me." He glanced around the interior. Slim stripes of light slanted through the vents along the ceiling.

She flicked a switch, electricity humming to life as they continued inside, away from the biting wind. "Is that really fair to you, though?"

"No worries, I can protect myself." He steered her toward a wall-long bench covered in a blue canvas cushion with little white anchors woven into the pattern.

She studied him through narrowed eyes as she sat. He settled beside her. Almost touching. His heart rate picked up with a prickly awareness of how tenuous the line was he was walking as he turned the conversation.

"Are you saying you want to be friends while you're working at the company?"

Friends?

Was that really what she thought he wanted? He was so aware of her—her scent, the way her skin softened under his fingers—that he could *feel* her, and they weren't even touching. He clenched his fingers into a fist to keep from reaching out to her. "I'm not sure anything platonic would work for us. But we didn't take time to become friends before."

"Then you're saying friends with benefits—because of the off-the-charts sex life?"

"Is that such a bad thing?"

He caught her gaze then. The electricity no longer just hummed in the boathouse lights. Instead, sparks danced between them, caught in the way neither of them could seem to look away. He saw conflicted feelings in her dark brown eyes. But also saw the longing. He just needed to be patient.

Naomi blinked, looking down. Breaking the moment between them. “I need to tell you something.”

His positive vibes faded. The hesitant tone in her voice didn’t bode well.

“You sound ominous.”

She bit her bottom lip again. “Chuck has looked at the numbers from the finance department regarding implementing your changes. We’re coming up short. We might not be able to fund the overhaul to the pipeline.”

A chill settled in his gut. The project he was passionate about—the tweak to the pipeline that would make the Alaska Oil Barons’ drilling more environmentally friendly—would go belly-up. All because he’d let himself believe what he’d wanted to believe. That he could work with Naomi, could justify stepping out of his solitary research and still hold on to his world while being a part of hers.

Now all that work was at risk. His time. His research. Everything he’d poured himself into for years.

The reality raked him raw. And it still didn’t hurt as much as knowing that—if what she was saying was true—he'd just lost his excuse to stay close to Naomi. That hurt more than anything.

Naomi tried to imagine a moment when this space, her suite, would feel normal and settled again. Or at least as sturdy as the timbers on the ceiling that reminded her of a ship's hull. A ship that could sail into a storm, unflinching.

She could use some of that bravado about now.

Winking sunlight filtered into the enclosed balcony that had been turned into a nursery, golden amber rays dusting the pink embellishments on the crib. Glints of light fractured as they struck the large crystalline bear on the top shelf of the bookcase. The bear had been in her family for as long as anyone could remember. At least something about this moment rang true. Constant. Familiar.

Carefully, Naomi plastered a smile onto her face as she removed the snow gear from her daughters. Mary was up first. Removing the outer layer, Naomi cooed at her, a new peace falling over her as she watched her baby suck on her fist.

Already, distinct personalities were forming. Mary hated the pacifier, preferring her fists. Anna loved to be held much more than her sister. Mary preferred to take in the world from a distance, content with her surroundings. Anna loved her pacifier, was a little fussier. After Naomi finished pulling the snow gear off Anna, she cradled each baby in an arm for a moment before settling them into the twin bassinet.

A snore interrupted her reverie. Naomi's gaze fell to the big Saint Bernard. Tessie slept in a dog bed by the window. Her brown-and-white fur glistened in the fading light.

Naomi's nerves were ragged after how the magical day had taken such a downward spiral. The walk with Royce had been fraught with tension, that explosive kiss and her dream lingering just below the surface for the whole outing, temptingly so.

Dangerous thoughts, especially when there was no denying he wanted her, too.

Except those feeling had him closing off from her. As the walk had ended, he'd shut down and shut her out. She should be glad for the distance, but her heart stung all the same, reminding her why they'd broken up in the first place…more than once. Moving from her feeling smothered to her worrying that he wanted her and the girls as a replacement for the fiancée and child he'd lost. Her worries that he couldn't thrive in her big, boisterous family.

There were too many ways a relationship between them didn't work. But that didn't stop her from wanting him more than breath.

Royce's knuckles drained of color as he gripped his key chain, she noticed. His free hand sought the small abacus on the ring, his fingers fidgeting with the device for a moment before he put the baby snowsuits in the laundry room on a hook to dry.

Searching for a way to disperse the awkward silence, she said, "I can take the girls down for dinner if you would prefer to hibernate up here."

"I'm not a bear. I can manage dinner with your family."

He was sure growling like a bear. His slick, all-black clothing hid nothing of his muscled physique. The power of his chest and arms temporarily distracted her.

But then, he had a reason to be grumpy, given the bombshell she'd dropped on him. It was selfish of her, since all the data wasn't in yet from running Chuck's numbers. She'd used the business excuse to create distance, and thereby caused him added worry. "I was just trying to be thoughtful. After all, you've given up your space for me and the girls."

"We could go to my place, if you're concerned about it."

His offer stopped her cold. It was tempting, and totally unworkable.

She gathered her thoughts for three heartbeats before she said, "We wouldn't fit."

Moving to his place would complicate everything even more. No. She needed to stay here. On her turf, her territory. Hold on to a semblance of power before she caved completely to the sensual pull of him. She recognized the push and pull between them, each trying to retain power in the situation, both strong-willed, both battling feelings they'd hoped were just temporary.

"A crib. A couple of car seats. I don't see the problem," he said, with a challenge in his eyes.

Was he trying to push her away? To bail because of what she'd told him? There was a time she would have sworn she could read him. Now, she lived in a constant state of confusion when it came to this man. "You can leave if you're ready. I would understand."

His strong jaw jutted. "I said I was staying until the gala, when your father returns, and I meant it."

The deep timbre of his voice filled the room and Tessie lifted her head from the dog bed with a low whimper.

"You're not obligated to stay." Naomi knelt beside the dog, threading her fingers through the silky soft fur.

"I gave you my word, and where you and the babies are is where I want to be." He walked to the twins' bassinet and gripped the edge.

"Is this situation getting you closure?" The words tumbled from her mouth, the ache in her chest deepening. "Because I'm not feeling it."

He glanced over his shoulder at her. "Naomi—"

"No." She couldn't play this game anymore. Not with the lump growing in her throat, pushing tears to her eyes. She needed to understand what the hell they were doing. "I'm not going to let you steamroll me or charm me or whatever your next plan is. This is so much more confusing than helpful. We're torturing ourselves—"

"Naomi, stop." He straightened from the bassinet.

"You and I want each other, there's no denying that. The attraction between us has been the one constant in our relationship and it isn't going away."

"Then put some distance between us. I don't want my daughters to be hurt because you're using them as surrogates for the child you lost."

"So you've said," he answered tightly. "I care about those girls enough not to do anything to hurt them. Listen when I say I'm not going anywhere—" A squawk from the bassinet had him turning back to the twins.

"Royce." Naomi strode toward him. "They're my daughters. I can handle this."

"Wait," he said, turning back toward her with Mary in his arms.

"What now?" She sighed in exasperation.

His gaze pinned hers. "I think Mary has a fever."

Nine

One step. Two steps. Three. Pivot and begin again.

Royce focused on the motion like a mantra in the examination area of the local emergency room. His fingers slid along his key chain abacus. But the ritual didn't bring much in the way of relief.

Each breath he drew revealed a new layer of pain and anxiety. His throat felt tight. Scenarios unfolded in his mind's eye, each more terrifying than the last.

He barely registered the whispers from the other side of the room as Delaney Steele and Glenna Mikkelson comforted Naomi, taking turns rubbing her back. Delaney's gaze met Royce's, her eyes soft with sympathy and support.

Soon they'd be discharged and could pick up the prescription.

Glancing over at Naomi again, he noticed the way her shoulders sank as her normally expressive, lithe body seemed to crumple in her oversize fringed cardigan as she cradled a baby in each arm.

Mary had a fever of 102 degrees Fahrenheit. Anna had a low-grade fever, as well. The doctor assured them the illness had nothing to do with the time outdoors. It was just a virus going around. But Royce couldn't help feeling guilty. Had he been so wrapped up in Naomi that he'd missed cues from the twins that they weren't feeling well?

They weren't cranky, though, just sleeping more.

Still, he felt like he'd failed them. Had failed Naomi.

Maybe he wasn't dad material. He'd been pushing his needs onto them, torturing himself and Naomi both because of proximity, temptation and abstaining. Now, it felt as if it was all imploding. With his work at the company in jeopardy anyway, all this—his reason for finding middle ground with Naomi—would be moot.

Their deadline, the gala, was only a little over a week away. After that, his work with the company would begin to pick up speed, provided the contract went through. He would return to his regular hours and wouldn't have this pseudo paternity leave.

A week left to forge some kind of connection that could last into the future. Or say goodbye forever.

Either way, time was running out to get his head together. He drew in a deep breath as he thrust his hands in his pockets to escape the slight chill of the air.

Naomi chewed a bottom lip, obviously rattled. Her hand trembled. Delaney gave her a hug, her reddish-brown hair obscuring her sister for a moment. He wanted to comfort Naomi, too, but she was deep in conversation with Delaney and Glenna.

Naomi's hair framed her slender face, those dark eyes filled with worry for the infants she held so protectively. "I know the doctor says the walk didn't cause this, but I still feel guilty. Why didn't I sense there was something off with them?"

Delaney wrapped her arm around her sister's shoulders. "If you'd stayed inside you would have been blaming yourself for not giving them enough fresh air and sunshine."

Glenna nodded, wisps of her blond hair falling out of her upswept bun. "You're a good mom. You're a careful mom. Babies get sick. It happens." She placed a manicured hand on Naomi's back.

Royce knew in his head that they'd both been careful with the babies. But in his heart? His gut?

A young doctor completing his residency came back into the room carrying a transparent clipboard, stethoscope slung around his neck. Boyish features made him seem impossibly young. As he opened his mouth to deliver an update, something seemed to halt his words.

Royce recognized that look. Calculation and observation became visible in his stare as he looked at Naomi. A longer pause. An assessment. The scientific process in action.

The doctor cleared his throat, his voice commanding much more authority than his young frame suggested. “Let’s get a temperature on you.”

Royce looked up sharply, understanding the doctor’s previous scrutiny. Naomi? Sick, too? How had he not noticed?

“What? I feel fine,” she insisted. “Just a little tired, which is normal. I have twins.” She twisted her hand in the air, a subtle protest echoed by her rings, as the turquoise-and-silver jewelry clinked together.

“Humor me.” The doctor held up the thermometer, waiting.

Naomi sighed, passed Mary and Anna to Delaney, then opened her mouth.

Royce watched the monitor. The numbers climbed…and stopped at 101.2. Ah, hell. He hadn’t missed just that the girls were ill. He’d been so wrapped up in having the hots for Naomi, he’d missed the signs that she was suffering, too.

The doctor looked in her mouth and ears quickly, then listened to her heart before nodding. “That virus bug has bit you, as well. Bed rest for all three of you.”

Royce knew it was just a routine illness, but his protective impulses fired full force. And a boatload of worry piled on top. These past weeks hadn't brought him any nearer to closure.

The time had only shown him how much of a hold Naomi still had over him.

Naomi had to admit there were times when a big family grated on her, but in moments of crisis, fatigue and trouble, gratitude filled her heart. She'd been so concerned with the twins, she'd failed to take care of her own body and focus on her own health. Thankfully, her younger sister and her sister-in-law were around, ready and willing to give her a much-needed reprieve. A night to practice self-care, sleep, become strong again.

Glenna and Delaney took Anna and Mary, stocked up with bottles of milk Naomi had expressed. Upon arriving at her suite, Naomi had made a beeline for the shower, where warm water caressed her aching muscles. She'd added an extra layer of indulgence to her routine by changing into winter silk pj's, and sinking into her sofa. She grabbed a burgundy cashmere blanket from a side basket, pulling it over her lap, enjoying the texture as it rubbed sensuously against exposed skin.

Royce had brought her a mug of chamomile tea with lemon before returning to the kitchen to heat up soup Delaney had sent.

And no question, Royce was the sexist "nurse" she'd ever met.

Vivaldi played in the background, and she let

her imagination spin with fantasies of waltzing with Royce, his strong arms around her, sweeping her off her feet.

Damn. If she hadn't known better, she would have sworn she was delirious with fever.

She hadn't even realized how bad she felt until the doctor noticed. She'd been so focused on the children. The ER physician had warned her that the viral infection could turn into something bacterial if she wasn't careful. Her immune system had been depleted by childbirth and caring for twins. She'd also been working even when tired.

And there was no denying her tumultuous relationship with Royce had worn her down. He was leaving soon. But saying goodbye and seeing him only occasionally at work wouldn't be any easier than facing him here every day.

She cupped the mug of hot tea in her hands, curling her legs up under the blanket.

Royce glanced over his shoulder. "How are you feeling?"

"Just tired. A little achy. Nothing major." She sipped the tea, the lemon and honey teasing her taste buds, which always seemed to be on hyperdrive around him, like the rest of her senses. "I hate that everyone's making such a fuss. I want to take care of my girls."

He turned toward her, carrying a tray with two bowls of Alaskan king crab chowder and fluffy wheat rolls. "If you run yourself down more, it'll be longer before you're on your feet. They're fine. They're here in the house being pampered to pieces by Glenna and Delaney. If they need you, you're only an elevator ride away."

"I know…it's just hard being away from them."

"Understandable." He set the tray on the coffee table, the creamy soup sending savory steam into the air.

Her heart stuttered with a hint of anxiety over feeling helpless, and the memories that brought up. "Thank you for all you've done."

"It's nothing," he said. "I just heated up what your sister sent."

"All the same, I still have problems with hospitals and being sick. It reminds me of the cancer treatments."

Royce skimmed his hand along her damp, braided hair. "Naomi…"

The images of days spent in hospitals vanished, replaced by other memories. Days with Royce, his touch. The way his mouth felt pressed into hers.

"It's okay. In the past." She leaned into the magic of his touch, which was intense. Too much so… She angled back and attempted to lighten the moment. "Maybe it was a blessing, after all, to have the babies in a car."

They shared a soft laugh, eyes connecting, the bond of that experience echoing between them. Then his dark eyes shifted, serious again. "The thought of what you went through as a teenager…"

"Hey, I'm okay now." She pulled her gaze away from his in case her eyes might betray the fear that sometimes still gripped her. She reached for a wheat roll and slathered it with butter. "I'm not even sure why I brought it up."

"I didn't mean to shut you down."

She waited for a moment, picking at the yeasty roll while Vivaldi's "Four Seasons" piped softly. Naomi wished she could eat, but having Royce this close to her without the distraction of the babies brought to mind all she'd been missing these last months. "Thank you for being there with me at the ER."

"Of course I was there. I was worried about them, too. Why would you doubt that?"

Of course he was worried about the girls. She felt small for the resentful feeling that thought brought. She shifted to a safer discussion. "Because of the problems at work. With the numbers not coming together for your project." A problem that, if unsolved, could end his connection to her, and she wouldn't have an excuse to see him at all.

Her stomach knotted tighter.

"That's business." He shrugged off her comment. "This is personal."

"But we were working on the personal in order to deal with being in the same work world." A task that was growing harder by the day with all the reminders of why she'd been drawn to him in the first place.

His eyes narrowed thoughtfully. "Are you saying you have a reason to keep my work out of the company?"

"No!" she exclaimed without hesitation. "God, no. I want your safety improvements on the pipeline to be implemented. I haven't given up. It's just going to be tougher than we first anticipated."

"Hey, it's okay, don't get wrought up. You should be taking it easy." He moved aside the dishes and adjusted the blanket on her lap, his hand lingering to palm her hip. "How about we put a pin in that conversation until we've both had a good night's sleep?"

She swallowed hard before continuing, "It's tough to think about anything other than the babies right now."

"Understandable. But they will be okay."

"I keep thinking if I hadn't taken them outside..."

"The doctor assured you their illness has nothing to do with our walk." He squeezed her hip lightly. "A virus just...happens. I'm more surprised that they both caught it at the same time."

She shifted back, tugging at the blanket until he got the message and pulled his hand away.

With an arrogant smile on his face.

She sat up straighter. "About Mary and Anna... I've learned not to question the twin connection. Brea and I even had our own twin language until we went to elementary school."

"And no one could understand what you were saying?"

She laughed softly. "Not a clue."

"The science of that is mind-boggling. The creation of a new language." His voice rumbled in the quiet room. "Watching them grow will be an adventure."

One he wouldn't be a part of. Her eyes stung. She blinked fast before looking up at him. "I'm sorry I didn't get things right when we were first together. I should have known it wasn't fair to let things move so fast, especially with kids involved. I never wanted to hurt you."

"We hurt each other." He stroked her face, then let his fingers continue down her throat to her collarbone. "Let's declare a truce for tonight."

She was tempted. So very tempted to take him up on that offer. Words dried up for a moment.

He tucked a knuckle under her chin and tipped her face to his until only a whisper of space separated them. If she swayed toward him even a hint…

Then she would be right back in the middle of a sea of desire that would lead to heartache, lead to losing herself in the kind of kiss between lovers who knew each other well and connected even when sex was out of the question.

The most dangerous kind of temptation of all.

For Naomi, the last two weeks were filled with forward motion. And yet she felt her emotional state slide back. Go to the past. To dangerous thoughts of Royce. Unarticulated futures. She was going through the motions, all right, and not making a damn bit of progress.

And yeah, the twins were fine. They'd made full recoveries. Their personalities continued to deepen and blossom.

But Naomi couldn't deny the pressure in the air between her and Royce. Knowing her struggle—and apparently determined to play meddling matchmaker—Delaney had encouraged Royce and Naomi to head out. Together. Alone. Under the guise of shopping for the girls, even though the very next day there'd be a baby shower at the Steele headquarters. Naomi had noticed that mischievous gleam in Delaney's dark brown eyes. Understood her sister's silent encouragement.

Yet here she was, enjoying an afternoon outing with him and the girls in a stroller at the Anchorage Museum. Playing with fire. Her chest tight with residual awareness and undeniable chemistry that she didn't know what to do with.

Right now, she and Royce were at a wary détente that only served to make willpower all the more difficult. Every day the desire to indulge in the mind-blowing attraction was damn near irresistible. Even a simple museum tour had her tied up in knots.

She couldn't stop herself from taking in the strong line of his jaw, the stubble as they moved through the Anchorage Museum.

A cluster of children holding museum maps sauntered by, being corralled by an overwhelmed looking young mother. She placed a hand on her hip, calling out to her group, attempting to draw the triplets' attention to the rotating cultural history exhibit. Naomi glanced at her babies sleeping in the stroller. She couldn't help but think of one day guiding her girls through here when they were older, seeing the wonder in their eyes as they took it all in.

"But, Mo-o-om, I want to go to the Earth and life science exhibit." One girl's bottom lip jutted out as she held up her hands in a state of total exasperation.

"We will, I promise. After this part," the mother cooed, steering her daughter toward the exhibit's entrance.

Naomi watched the scene, her smile deepening. She leaned against Royce, felt the slight heat radiating from his body as she whispered, "I can envision you as a kid with one of those little science kits, mixing chemicals and making an overflowing volcano."

"Actually, I wanted to be a football star."

His deadpan delivery caught her off guard. Lowered her defenses. She couldn't stop herself from drinking in the sight of him in well-worn jeans and a cable knit sweater. He wore his wealth so casually, a man comfortable in his skin with no need to flaunt his success.

She pulled her attention back to the conversation. "A football player? Really?" she asked, surprised that Royce would have ever considered such a career path.

"Hell, no. Too many people."

Laughing, she pulled him toward the rotating art exhibit, passing by the windowpanes that showcased glimpses of the city. Of her fair state. "So you built volcanoes, after all."

"Actually, I wanted to be either an astronaut or a zookeeper."

"Wow, that's a surprise. A fun one, though. I can see it, and it's endearing."

Royce grimaced. "Endearing? That's not what I was going for."

"You do just fine giving off the brooding vibe. It's okay to let people have a peek inside every now and again."

"I don't want to argue with you." He took her hand in his.

"Okay then." She linked their fingers. "I want to hear more about Royce the Zookeeper. What derailed you from your path?"

"I realized I couldn't take them all with me out into the woods."

"Valid point. And the astronaut dream?"

He quirked an eyebrow at her. "I might not have come back?"

She squeezed his hand while staring into his eyes, the crowd around them fading so that all she saw was this man. "How did we never talk about this before?"

"We didn't do a lot of talking back then. Remember?"

Heat washed over her at the shared memory. Especially knowing he was thinking about the same things she was. Tearing off each other's clothes. Tasting and touching. Feasting.

She swallowed hard. Maybe she looked as breathless as she felt, because Royce smiled with just a hint of male satisfaction before he guided her to sit on a bench by a display of Inuit art that made Naomi think of her grandmother. Nights spent by a fire as a child enthralled by the oral history of half her soul.

"And what about you, Madame Lawyer?" Royce asked. "Childhood career dreams?"

She was grateful for the redirection. They didn't need to wander down those old paths again, as tempting as it might be to simply lose herself in his touch. Drawing a deep breath, she reached back in her memories.

"I wanted to start a glacier wedding business, complete with all the plane rides out to the remote location to say their vows."

"For real?" He leaned back on the bench, his arms spread wide so that one lay close to her back. Almost touching.

With an effort, she forced her thoughts back to the conversation.

"Absolutely. Uncle Conrad got married in a glacier wedding when I was in elementary school. I thought it was the most romantic thing ever." She could picture the perfect crispness even now. Feel the icy wind on her cheek. Remembered the way the Milky Way had provided a backdrop even princesses in a fairy tale would envy.

"What stopped you?"

"He got divorced and I decided glacier weddings were like a *Titanic* jinx."

Royce winced. "Ouch."

"I had a lot of fun with the idea for a while, though. I dressed up my siblings for the occasion."

Hoisting herself up from the bench, Naomi pushed the stroller as she circled around one of the installations, taking in the details of the painting of a fishing village. Remembering the way her grandmother had supplied all sorts of clothes for her business.

"My grandmother was on board. Anything to make me happy. She had a chest full of clothes I was allowed to use. Delaney always enjoyed playing dress-up and performing the ceremonies. Broderick says he hated it, but to be honest, that's not how I remember it. I'd make us all walk into the wood's edge for the ceremony. Dad never liked us being by the water. Always afraid something would happen to us."

A lump filled her throat. The memory of her sister ached in her bones. Even now, placing Breanna in memories felt like a private act. Something that would recede if Naomi shared too much. Selfishly, she kept her deceased sibling's role to herself.

"That's quite a memory," he said.

"There are photos. I've used them to shut up a big-mouth sibling on more than one occasion."

"And then you turned your back on romance."

"Not romance. Just weddings." Suddenly she became very aware of her pulse. The touch of his fingertips to hers. And the silence. "I even did some freelance work last year helping people edit their online dating profiles."

"The romance dream lives on. Perhaps your glacier wedding dream can come back to life, too."

The wry tone in his voice gave her pause. Was it just a dream that they were rediscovering something between them here? Something romantic? Something more than explosive chemistry and opposing views of the world? He had losses and deep feelings, and so did she. She'd grieved for her sister and her mother. She'd blamed Royce for not moving on, but maybe she'd had a hard time moving on and trusting, too.

Could they forge a true connection? One that would allow them to grieve for their pasts together? One that would last?

Outside the Steele boardroom, Royce braced himself for a killer confrontation.

Hordes of family and friends were throwing a baby shower.

He took a deep breath, steadying himself. Thankfully, the great windowpanes bathed the room in natural light. Made the space feel more open and encompassing.

He stood next to the tall, suave Birch Montoya. The man reminded him of old Hollywood films, bourbon and cigars. They stood in the reception area near the glass wall that separated the entry from the boardroom. Muffled noises ensued, punctuated by shrieks of women's laughter.

Apparently, the party was already under way.

Beer in hand, he stayed by Chuck, Broderick and Birch. Half paying attention to the conversation, half taking in the scene.

The men flocked around the small table covered with food. Chuck tossed shrimp onto his plate. With a Viking-like build and complexion, he exuded a sense of power.

Royce leaned back, peering through the doorway to where the women were gathered. The blue chairs that normally flanked the table had been rearranged into scattered semicircles. Perfect for small group chats.

There was no denying the elegance of this event. Pink and white balloons were clustered here and there. And although it was winter, spring seemed to have exploded in the room. So many flowers. He recognized roses and lilies, but not the other blooms poking through the central arrangement.

A time capsule in the shape of a baby bottle had been placed at the entrance for attendees to write to the twins. They'd crack that sucker open on their eighteenth birthday. A nice idea, really.

Would he be a distant memory to them then? Even a memory at all?

He couldn't help the way his eyes trailed after Naomi. Taking in her curves in that short pink dress with brown tights. The way her fringed boots seemed to deepen her mystique, accentuating her knack for bringing eclectic textures and threads together.

He watched the way she straightened the ceiling-high stack of presents. Careful, he realized, to keep them from falling on the elaborate cake. And what a cake it was—an icing creation of twin polar bear cubs in mittens and hats. Extravagant.

He was thankful she felt well enough to celebrate. Even knowing she was healthy now, he couldn't help but think about time closing in on them to end this togetherness experiment. He needed to accept that she knew her limits. Naomi had always been a workaholic. Her dynamo personality was only one of the many things that drew him to her. He'd been so determined to find closure, and somehow this time with her and the girls had only made the prospect of losing her all the worse.

Breaking his stare, he placed a chicken salad croissant on his plate. Passed over the chocolate fondue fountain, nuts and shish kebab fruit.

Jack stood at the wet bar, his still jet-black mustache making his white teeth seem even brighter.

Wiggling his fingers, Jack paused indecisively, hand oscillating over a mimosa and a beer, avoiding the sparkling water altogether. “Great shindig to celebrate the twins.”

“A nice way to celebrate everyone getting over that virus.” Royce took a swig of his beer—the Steele-Mikkelson brand, Icecap Brews—letting the hoppy flavor linger on his tongue. If only the merger of the two oil businesses could be as easy as the new joint ownership of their two merged small breweries. “It’s good to have you back.”

The timing of the shower had been scheduled to accommodate Jack and Jeannie’s return.

Jack nodded, his eyebrows expressive. He crossed his hands over his chest, compressing the flannel fabric as he continued, “Good to see those babies again. FaceTime didn’t do them justice.”

“And your honeymoon?”

Jack paused once more, looking up at the material that covered the ceiling. For a moment, Royce wondered what it was. Chiffon? Tulle? Was there a difference?

“Well…” Naomi’s dad scooped up some peanuts and shifted them in his fist. “Jeannie and I are family people. That’s part of what drew us to each other. But the time away was good for us. No work. A rarity for me, but I’m a convert.”

“You’re really going to retire?”

“Semiretire. Jeannie and I will both be on the Alaska Oil Barons board through the transition.

After that, we'll see." The older man pinned Royce with a contemplative stare. "How are you and Naomi?"

He wanted to stay present. Not think about their budding connection that went beyond the physical, or how much he would give for one last time with her in his bed, or how nothing had really changed.

Or worst of all, their looming goodbye.

But still, Naomi kept crossing his mind. His eyes kept searching for her.

Angling more to the left, Royce kept her in his line of vision. Naomi stood with some of the employees. The new assistant, Milla, laughed as baby songs were played and excited participants shouted out the name of the mystery tune.

All the men watched the commotion from afar. These baby songs were not nearly as inventive or creative as Royce's periodic table lullaby. But whatever. Time to focus again.

And stop avoiding Jack's question about Royce's relationship with Naomi. "We're taking care of the girls."

Not untrue. The answer betrayed nothing of his feelings. Or her feelings, the ones he couldn't read.

Jack narrowed his gaze. "You've gotta admit it's unusual for exes to spend this much time together."

"Like I said, we're here for the girls."

"I understand how deep the love can be for kids. It's about more than a biological bond… But is that all this is? For both of you? Because if one of you is hoping for more, this is going to go bad fast."

"I understand you care about your daughter. But this is between Naomi and me." Royce set his plate down on a nearby table. Sometimes his quiet nature, his calling as a researcher, gave off the wrong impression. He had a helluva backbone and he knew how to use his voice. "How about we discuss work. I hear my projcct is at risk due to financing."

Chuck and Birch sidled closer, as if sensing the tension. Their posturing was somehow softened by the presence of Mary and Anna's pictures on a makeshift clothesline in the foreground.

Seeing Chuck reminded Royce about the whole numbers-crunch mess. He hadn't planned on bringing that up here. Now. But it beat the hell out of talking about his relationship with Naomi. And bottom line, if he wanted time to figure out the answers, to decide if they even had a future, he needed to keep his "in" with Alaska Oil Barons, Inc. "Any progress on retooling the numbers for the pipeline upgrades?"

Chuck's eyebrows shot up. "I guess I shouldn't be surprised Naomi read you in on that," he said with a tight jaw. "Business loyalty has always been iffy around here."

Royce bristled and Broderick didn't look much happier. Jack stepped between them. "This isn't the time. We're not going to ruin Naomi's baby shower." He turned to his son. "You and Glenna are the CFOs. Set a meeting." It was an order. No mistaking it.

So much for the older man backing off and letting the next generation take over. Things were coming to a head. Fast.

Getting Royce's designs into actual production on this project could have ripple effects worldwide. An affordable solution to prevent disasters—like oil spills—was groundbreaking. And yeah, for a scientist like him to be remembered for that kind of contribution was a definite plus.

This deal falling through meant the end of those particular aspirations. It would mean the loss of more than a year of work. But when he thought about leaving, it wasn't losing the work that made Royce's chest feel like he'd just taken a sucker punch. It was losing Naomi and the girls.

And Royce had less than a week until the gala to lock this down, one way or another.

Ten

Time was running out.

Sitting on the floor by Tessie's dog bed, moonlight bathing the babies in a hazy glow, Naomi thumbed through photos on her phone, scrolling back from the day the twins were born to her baby shower. Six weeks had passed in the blink of an eye since the snowstorm delivery. The date for the gala for her father and Jeannie was just around the corner.

And her time with Royce as the girls' "nanny" was drawing to a close.

She threaded her fingers through Tessie's silky fur with one hand, phone clutched in the other as she scrolled past another photo. The babies were asleep.

Royce had gone for a trek in the woods to clear his head after a large family supper.

So quickly, her device storage had transitioned from a repository of memes and Alaskan scenery to images of Anna and Mary. A chronicle of their first few weeks of life. An amazing technological advancement, really.

She stopped for a moment to look at a picture of Anna and Mary bundled up in the sleigh, Royce standing protectively in the background, legs braced against the wind. Her heart panged. All her stories, all her memories of feeling like a mother, placed him in proximity. Royce wasn't someone she could easily rend from her life. From the way she understood herself.

It wasn't just the photos. No. His impact was so much more than that. Everywhere she looked there were visible, material traces of their cohabitation, round two. His globe found residence on the bookcase next to her grandmother's map of Alaska. His gloves were lying near the twins' snowsuits and hats. Everywhere, reminders. Everywhere, places she'd notice an absence if he left.

When he left.

Leaning forward, she reached for his MIT pullover hanging from the doorknob. She brought the fleece to her face and inhaled the scent of him. As if she could ever forget. Every facet of him was imprinted in her mind.

Saying goodbye would be tough. Breaking things

off, but still seeing him, felt equally as painful. These weeks together had made her decision only more difficult as she felt the joy of being around him, felt his love for her daughters and saw his tension ratchet up at the large family gatherings. No matter which way she turned, there was heartbreak.

Was it wrong of her to want to hold tight to these last days together?

Hell, where was her spine, her grit, her take-charge spirit?

She brought his pullover to her face again, breathed in the scent of him and let it swirl around inside her, arousing and intoxicating. Her body came to life, waking from the recovery slumber of the past six weeks. Her need for him flamed back to life as her body reclaimed her sensuality.

More specifically, her sensual need for *this* man.

She might not be able to have everything she wanted—a future—with Royce. They were both too wounded from their past losses. They both just had too much baggage between them. But she could make the most of her week left with him to say good-bye before she moved on with her life.

Royce had expected to work like hell to get closer to Naomi during their last week together before the party.

Staring at the trail of rose petals leading through the living room toward the master bath, he had a feeling she was ahead of him on this.

He had no idea what had changed her mind about sleeping together again. She hadn't mentioned anything about being together again long term and he couldn't deny there would be emotional fallout from any sexual encounter.

And still he didn't intend to argue with her.

This was what he'd wanted. To be in her bed—or shower—again. To be with her.

Anticipation ramped higher. Hotter. He shrugged out of his parka and boots, following the petals. His steps crushed the blooms and launched microbursts of perfume into the air. He considered ditching all his clothes, but he needed to hear the words from her lips first. Her plans. Her wants.

He rapped his knuckles against the door. It creaked open, as if left ajar just for him. He stepped inside, the sound of the shower greeting him, along with soft jazz music.

She'd once told him the luxury bathroom was her haven, from the spa tub to the oversize Swedish shower with water jets along the sides as well as overhead.

However, those didn't draw his attention nearly as much as the woman.

Steam filled the shower stall, her body a sexy silhouette. The small stone fireplace nearby glowed with flames, a decorative pot of potpourri simmering over the blaze.

"Care to join me?" Her voice rode the steam, sending a bolt of desire straight through him.

Hell, yes.

"Where are the babies?" He should have thought to check before following the rose trail.

Naomi skimmed her fingers down the glass, streaking away steam, before pushing the door open. "Delaney is watching them for a few hours."

Was she already shifting from his help to her family's? A quick thought, an unsettling possibility, but one he brushed aside as swiftly as his clothes.

Eyes locked on her face, her curves, he closed the space between them. His feet soaked up the warmth of the heated floor. Then he had her in his arms again, her body flush against his. No words were necessary. He knew her. She knew him. His mouth found hers, familiar and new all at once.

It had been too long. Water sluiced over them as his tongue swept hers, touching and tasting. Desire pulsed through him, so intense his hands shook. He needed to stay in control. To go carefully with her.

He cupped her face, his forehead resting on hers. Maybe some words were needed, after all. "Did the doctor give you any restrictions I should know about?"

Naomi scored her nails lightly down his back, then sank them into his hips. "She said I'm cleared for all activities, only no trapeze." Naomi paused, arching against him. "I'm just supposed to listen to my body."

The teasing look in her eyes made his breath

catch. Hold. His hands skimmed her slick skin, settling at the indentation of her waist.

"And what is your body telling you?" He'd missed this playfulness they'd once shared so easily.

"That I want your touch." She kissed his mouth, his jaw, nipped his collarbone. "That I need you. I need this—and I think you do, too."

Desire roared hotter than the steam heat of the shower.

"Damn, but you are gorgeous." His words were a husky growl.

She pressed closer, her hips arching toward his before she looked up at him through eyelashes holding droplets of water. "And you sure know how to make a new mom feel good about herself."

Seeing her this way, being with her again, was a gift he would not waste. A gift beyond measure.

"You've always been beautiful." He cradled the weight of her breasts in his hands, his thumbs circling her hardening nipples. "But now you are even more incredible. You're turning me inside out."

He tracked the way her pupils dilated. The way her head rolled back with pleasure at this touch.

"Glad to know." Her words were a breathless rush, her lashes fluttering. "The feeling's so very mutual. It's been far too long."

Damn straight. Hunger for her all but overwhelmed him. "Give me a minute to get to my shaving kit for—"

"A condom?" She pulled the packet from behind

the shampoo, one step ahead of him on this, too. “I saw them there. A clue that you were hoping, too.”

“Always.” Sliding aside the damp length of her hair, he trailed kisses down her throat. Tasted her skin scented with lavender soap.

She tore open the packet and sheathed the hot, pulsing length of him. Taking her time. Teasing a response from him. But after so long without her, without this, her touch threatened to send him over the edge. He took her hands in his and lifted them over her head, to the tile wall, the warm spray showering them from all directions.

He slid into her slowly, carefully, his eyes on her every moment, watching. Willing her to feel his caring, the restraint.

She rolled her hips, drawing him deeper. “I’m okay. More than okay. Being with you…” Her breath hitched. “It’s everything.”

Passion, the physical connection, had never been in question. Their bodies were in sync. Even more so having been lovers who knew exactly what made the other melt with need.

He’d been drawn to her from the moment he first saw her. Unwillingly drawn, but unmistakable. This connection between them didn’t make sense, but it was undeniable. The clamp of her around him, the slick glide as her body welcomed his in a way that made him never want to leave.

She swayed, then looped her arms more securely around his neck. In seamless response, he anchored her against the tile wall, whispering his desire in her ear, his breath hot against her neck.

Steam filled the oversize stall, blotting out the rest of the room…the rest of the world. Moisture in the air carrying the scent of lavender and their mingled perspiration.

A heady perfume.

Desire simmered hotter and hotter, the flames building, stoked by the feel of her breasts in his hands, her hands on him. Until he was close. So close to the edge. He tucked his hand between them, helping ease her toward her release.

Remembering. Wanting more of her.

Her breath caught just before her neck arched, a moan sliding between her lips. He caught the sound with his mouth as he thrust to his own release, the power rocking through him with an intensity even beyond his dreams. And his dreams had been mighty damn intense.

He held her against him, bracing her as the aftershocks of her release rippled through her. Then in a fluid move, he slid his hands under her bottom and lifted her against him as he turned to sit on the shower bench. He settled her across his lap, holding her, her head resting on his chest.

He'd missed her, missed this, missed so much about being with her in the months apart after their breakup.

How could she have changed his life so monumentally in less than a year?

Something found so fast could be taken away just as quickly.

As he drew in gasps of humid air, he couldn't stop his mind from traveling back. To how when she'd needed him most, he'd let her down. She'd been put on bed rest for her blood pressure and he'd overreacted. Gone into overprotective mode. Damn near smothered her, when her free spirit was one of the things he admired most about her. He of all people should understand her need for space.

Why the hell couldn't they get this right?

He didn't know the answer to that. But one thing shone through.

He wasn't giving up searching just because of some artificial deadline at a party.

Even the smallest movements felt alive with a new, visceral energy.

And yes, it had everything to do with the rekindled romance between her and Royce. Naomi pushed aside her doubts, resolving to enjoy this last week together and not think about goodbyes.

Leaning against the kitchen countertop just before midnight, she hungrily took him in as a growl erupted from her stomach. Many kinds of feasts were present here.

Royce's jeans hung low on his hips, his chest bare and calling to her fingers to explore. Her skin tingled under her winter silk pajamas. She hadn't doubted her decision to make love in the shower, but she had been nervous about showing her post-delivery body.

A concern he'd dispelled.

And she'd also been a hint apprehensive there might be discomfort, in spite of the doctor's assurance that she'd healed.

A concern Royce had also ousted with his tender, patient lovemaking that added an extra layer of steam to the shower.

The girls were settled in their bassinet and she should go to sleep soon or it would be a long, bleary-eyed day tomorrow. But she planned to make one more memory tonight to tuck away.

Perhaps she played with fire here.

Part of that statement felt literal as they assembled the chocolate fondue and fruit spread. Sweets and junk food were Royce's guilty pleasure and she'd made sure to order his favorite indulgences. Strawberries, blueberries and apple slices filled the trough around the chocolate fountain.

Bluegrass music provided a tempo to their movements as they prepared the meal. Notes that occasionally inspired Royce to grip her tightly, making her heart flutter.

Tessie watched thoughtfully, careful as she swept across the floor. Naomi tossed the Saint Bernard a soup bone. The dog graciously accepted the treat, circling before sprawling out.

Naomi rinsed her hands. "It's strange how many things I didn't notice while we were together."

"Such as?"

"I can't seem to recall you having a hobby for your free time."

Shrugging, Royce picked up the bowl of strawberries. "I like my work. Besides, you're one to talk. You live for your work, too." He ran water over the strawberries, then patted them dry.

She stared at him, waiting for the answer.

"I hike, I ride, I camp—any number of things out in the wilds."

She grinned. "Where it's quiet, with little risk of other people showing up?"

"I'm not a total hermit. I just prefer to avoid large crowds." He tossed the hand towel over his shoulder again.

"I like the outdoors, too, and experiencing that with others." She stirred the melting chocolate, until the lumps smoothed into a creamy blend. "When the girls are old enough, I'll show them all the places I went with my family."

"And camp there, too?" He popped a strawberry in his mouth, his gaze dropping to hers.

How was it a movement so simple could make her heart beat faster?

"Maybe. If they want to." She parted her lips as he brought a chocolate berry to her mouth.

His thumb stroked briefly, the slightest of touches, and still the connection flared hot between them before his hand slid away.

"Why the hesitation?"

She chewed, the taste exploding in her mouth. Everything about this man made her moan. “I can’t recreate the past, and they deserve to make their own memories.”

“Is that another dig at you thinking I don’t have my past resolved?”

“It would only feel like a dig if it were true. You would know that better than me,” she blurted. Damn. She closed her eyes for a moment before continuing, “Why are you still so good to me?”

“You deserve it.”

“A lot of people deserve it.” She stirred an apple wedge in the chocolate, leaning one hip against the cool granite counter. “My head’s spinning here.”

He clasped her waist, stilling her fidgeting. “You think I’m not over my ex and losing the baby.”

“Never mind. Forget I brought it up. I’m wrecking a wonderful evening.” She brought the fudge-covered apple slice to his mouth.

He took the fruit, licking the last drop from her fingertip. Shivers of awareness skittered down her spine.

Warmed chocolate and fruit.

Juices from the strawberry stained her hands. She licked her fingers, watching his eyes dilate with desire. Then Royce brushed against her, the muscles of his back rippling as he dipped fruit into the chocolate fountain.

He pushed aside the neckline of her shirt and drew the tip of the berry along her shoulder, leaving a barely there trail of warm chocolate. He ducked his head and kissed the sweetness from her skin.

She melted more than the chocolate, losing herself in the flick of his tongue against her skin. Memories of their lovemaking racked her again, rekindling her desire. She wanted more from this man, here and now. She ran her fingers over his chest, savoring the flex of his muscles, his awareness of her touch.

Her hand slid down, along the waistband of his jeans, finding the hard length of him, curving to fit and stroke. His low growl of approval reverberated in the space between them. Naomi parted her legs, inviting him to step closer, an invitation he quickly accepted. She thrummed with passion, her body crying out for him so tangibly she could swear her ears rang with it. Louder, until she realized—

The fire alarm was wailing.

The blare hammered through the tender moment. Followed by the cries of the babies waking.

Panic surged. Thankfully, Naomi's feet moved faster. She raced to pull clothes on. Her protective mothering instincts notched into overdrive. A quick pivot on her heel, and she took off for the nursery, Royce right behind her.

Tessie whined and barked, urging them to move faster. Faster. Hands fumbled to secure her daughters in warm clothes. Not knowing how much time they had, Royce brought thick blankets.

They moved together as if the plan to see Anna and Mary to safety silently sounded between them.

Anna cried in Naomi's arms as they made their way to the staircase, past the fireplace.

Another sharp bark came from Tessie as they descended the stairs. As they reached the bottom floor, a wafting hint of smoke sent her fear higher. This wasn't a false alarm.

Chaos filled the house. Naomi barely registered the other members of her family rushing outdoors. Thank God Royce had been with her. She couldn't miss how quick he was in a crisis. How steady and secure.

Naomi couldn't say the biting cold of the Alaskan night burned against her cheeks, sending a shock to her system.

No. That wasn't it.

It was the sight of her younger sister, whose rich brown hair contrasted against the paleness of her mostly bare skin. Delaney wrapped in a cream-colored quilt really woke her up.

Mostly, it was who *else* shared that quilt. Birch Montoya.

Naomi couldn't decide what to make of that sight. And even more confusing?

Her sister and Birch were so different, so oppositional, that friction happened just from them being in the same room. So why were they huddled under the quilt together, a smirk on Birch's face, a satisfied secret smile on Delaney's?

Was it the same with Naomi and Royce?

She'd been so convinced they were wrong for

each other and that all she felt was just lust or infatuation. So why was he the first person she turned to in a crisis?

And why was she so reluctant to let him go?

Eleven

Royce cradled the infant to his chest, his heart still jack hammering.

When the fire alarm went off, his first thought had been of Naomi and the girls. A gut-wrenching flash of what his life would be like if something happened to them.

And the pain damn nearly tore him in half.

Smoke tightened the knot of dread, triggering memories of that fatal accident years ago.

Just as fast, he'd pushed those distracting thoughts aside and focused on getting them all out of the house. Only to find it was a false alarm.

The aftermath of the adrenaline surge still scoured his veins. He forced even breaths in and out of his mouth, holding Mary while Naomi cradled Anna.

His breaths puffed in the night air as they waited for the house to clear. His mind spun with what-ifs that still haunted him. What if they hadn't pushed that first traffic light? Instead of gunning through on the yellow, he could have slowed. Been steady. Been more reactive and reflexive.

Had his inability to stop at the warning yellow light indicated a default in his ability to take care of the ones he cared for? Was that really why his former fiancée had left after the miscarriage and accident?

More important…was he now a ticking time bomb?

And could he forgive himself if lightning struck his life again?

Damn, but the past was a dogged beast. He drew in another icy breath and looked around, grounding himself in the present. He wasn't surprised to see the family in nightclothes. He was, however, stunned to see Birch Montoya with Delaney, both disheveled.

Even in the dim light of the stars and moon, Delaney's blushed cheeks were visible. Likely a combo of embarrassment and the chill. "Sorry, everyone. The fireplace flue got stuck and we couldn't put out the flames before the smoke set off the detectors," she said.

The throng of family fanned smoke through the open doors as Naomi and Royce stayed back with the twins, keeping them away from the noxious air.

"Um, Delaney..." Naomi kept her voice low. "You and Birch Montoya? An item? Did I just step into the set for *Sleeping with the Enemy*?"

Royce wondered the same thing, but at least the attention was on someone else, giving him and Naomi a break from questions about their plans.

But even as the sisters exchanged glances, Royce's mind slid to his next dilemma, rocking Mary in his arms. She gurgled a little, a smile on that rosebud mouth. What if that fire alarm had been real? If there'd been a legitimate crisis? If the babies and Naomi had been alone and asleep with a real fire raging through the house?

The possibility struck too close to his past.

He felt his heart tightening again at all that he'd lost. His unborn child and fiancée. The ache was so intense he forced himself to shut it down and focus on the present.

Delaney quirked an eyebrow at her sister. "I thought you liked Birch."

"I do," Naomi answered, her fingertip grazing Royce's arm. Sending him not into the normal wave of passion, but back to the moment of the accident. To the moment he'd lost it all. "You're the one who paints his business practices as evil incarnate. Although this—" she gestured toward Birch "—whatever it is, it definitely isn't business."

"We've been on again, off again for a while now," Delaney admitted. "We're just not so sure we won't get egged on by our friends if we go out in public together."

Naomi's laughter grabbed his attention again.

"Since when did our parents bring us up to bow to peer pressure?"

"My friends share my values."

Naomi angled in to say softly, "But you're totally hot for him."

"You're one to talk about having conflicted feelings for the guy you're sleeping with." She nodded toward Royce.

Royce winced. But then the truth was unavoidable. He nudged Naomi. "We should get the babies back up to the room and away from the smoke."

"Of course." Naomi pointed to her sister. "But we'll talk later."

"Uh-huh. Sure," Delaney said with a dismissive shake of her head, before she rejoined the smoke-waving effort.

Maneuvering away from the family, Royce felt another weight slam through him. This time not from the past, though, but rather from the present—Birch Montoya. Sending a quick glance over his shoulder, he picked out Birch's silhouette, a thought tugging at him, persisting even when the rest of Naomi's family faded from sight.

"Is something wrong?" Naomi asked, as they took the elevator back to her suite.

"The numbers," Royce answered, still chasing

the notion through his mind. If he was right, at least there'd still be time to intervene.

"What do you mean?"

He leaned back in the elevator as the doors slid closed. "For the upgrades to the pipeline. Montoya is made of money and yet his bid for something he says he wants to help promote comes in just short."

Naomi gasped. "You think he's gaming the system? Using my sister for insider tips?"

The pain in her voice for her sibling couldn't be missed. All the more reason to figure out the truth sooner rather than later.

"I like the guy, so it bugs the hell out of me even considering this." Royce wasn't one to make friends lightly. "It also bothers me that my gut instinct may have been wrong. But something's off and he doesn't exactly have a reputation for bending over backward to save the planet."

"True… I'll talk to Glenna and Broderick about looking more closely at how the data was disseminated." She frowned as the doors slid open. "But God, I hope it's not true, for Delaney's sake. Not that I think he's right for her, given how different they are. But to be betrayed that way…" She shook her head. "I just hope it's not true."

Her flat assessment that Montoya and Delaney weren't right for each other caught Royce right in the midsection. He couldn't avoid the natural conclusion. The parallel.

If Naomi believed Birch and Delaney's differences should keep them apart, then in spite of what Royce and Naomi had shared earlier tonight, they were finished.

Milla watched the Steele family from the icy woods as they went back into the mansion. Although she remained hidden, huddling in the pine branches, she still held her breath. As if a loud exhalation might give away her position. Compromise the whole operation.

A silly thought, maybe. But still one she couldn't shake. Not when Milla's future mingled in with the success of her mission. Which meant remaining hidden in the trees until the mansion settled back down.

She'd taken a risk tonight coming to the sprawling waterside home. It had been a silly, frivolous indulgence. Like the night she'd sneaked into the hospital under the guise of delivering flowers. But coming to Anchorage at all had been a risk. A risk she was willing to take—if it paid off.

Maybe she'd gotten overly confident these past weeks with her success at leaking data to the Florida investor. The stock shares had adjusted as she'd hoped. The pipeline innovations were all but a no-deal, which would be a huge blow to the Steele-Mikkelson merger into Alaska Oil Barons, Inc.

Wind whipped and trees moaned in response, the scent of smoke heavy on the breeze. She pulled her ponytail tighter, letting out a deep, satisfied breath as the door of the mansion finally shut. Remaining crouched, she felt a smirk tug at her mouth.

Through the thin gloves, Milla could feel the texture of the bark as she counted her successes. Her almost-compromised successes.

But she'd made the mistake of being greedy for a bigger win. For revenge. She'd used the excuse of dropping off papers to stop by the house, telling Broderick she would show herself out.

She'd sneaked into the study to see if the family portrait was still in place, the one of the entire clan before the airplane crash—easy enough to do, since she knew the layout of the house. Except Delaney and Birch had come into the room for their sneaky affair. She'd barely had time to hide in the nook behind the grandfather clock.

A favorite hiding place from Steele childhood days.

Yes, the Mikkelsons had to pay for all they'd taken.

Clutching the nursery monitor, Naomi padded back into the living area, where Royce was putting away the chopped fruit.

The man worked with such precision an automaton would be jealous. And while restoring order had its charm, she realized by his restricted movements and the tightness hinging in his lower jaw that Royce had yet to settle. He seemed to crackle, he was so visibly upset. As he had been ever since the fire alarm went off. She just wasn't sure if the cause was the pipeline discussion or the safety scare with the smoke.

Either way, their romantic evening was officially wrecked.

Logic told her the best approach would be to go to sleep, then discuss their concerns with a clear head in the morning. But the restlessness inside her, the raw emotions from their lovemaking earlier, pushed her impulsive nature to the fore. The silence weighed between them, cut only by the hum of the baby monitor and the dog's light snore.

Tension inched higher, along with the ache for things to be different between them. Easier. For Royce to walk over to her, sling an arm around her shoulders as they went to bed together. But still he kept his broad back to her.

Hadn't they flirted with that version of their lives just a few short hours ago?

As much as she wanted to be with him again before their time together ended, she'd been through the pain of losing him before. Soon, her daughters would grow closer to him and feel that pain, too. And the more she delayed it, the worse it would be. He'd helped her—for whatever reasons of his own—and the time had come for her to stand on her own.

She joined him in the kitchen, leaning against the granite countertop, just like earlier. Though everything felt different now. "No one is making you stay."

Placing the fruit in the refrigerator, he glanced sideways at her, his handsome face inscrutable. "For someone who's such a fighter, you sure do quit easily."

"I just think we're delaying the inevitable." Even as she said it, she couldn't help hoping he had a magic reason ready for why this time would be different. A too-familiar lump formed in her throat.

She'd picked a helluva time for this discussion.

"Just like that, you're through?" he asked, his gaze unflinching, unreadable.

"The whole reason for this nanny experiment was to gain closure, since we would be working together. That's unlikely now." She clenched her hands in front of her, resisting the urge to shout at him to fight for her. "The money isn't there for your work to be implemented with our company."

"You want me to take the research elsewhere?" Still, he didn't touch her. Didn't deny what she'd said about *them*.

He took a step closer, as if he might reach for her. Her heart fluttered.

Yes. Perhaps now. Was this the start of the fight for her? He didn't draw any nearer; his arms dangled at his sides.

"Of course I don't." She bit her lip, tears welling. Not that she would let them fall. If she cried, he would try to comfort her and that would only make this tougher. "But it's your life's work. Business is business. Delaney will probably join you, anyway."

A flash of pain shot through his eyes, the first sign this was hurting him, too. "We are more than the sum of our work." He rested his hands on her shoulders, that touch she'd craved. His fingertips felt at once foreign and familiar. "This isn't about business. This is about you and me and the kids being a family."

"A family." Her breath hitched on the word, her emotions churning as he offered that morsel of hope. Still, she couldn't ignore the gut-deep fear that he was using her and her daughters as substitutes for what he'd lost before. There'd been no evidence to the contrary. Naomi could not divorce her lawyer sensibilities in this manner. "You say this is about being a family. Where does being a couple fit in?"

"You and the girls are a package deal."

True, but she wanted more from him. Needed more from him. "I should be grateful you aren't running screaming in the opposite direction from a single mom with newborn twins." Her voice rose with each word. She flattened her palms on his chest. Feeling so emotionally vulnerable after making love to him, she had to fight against putting up a wall, and his prickliness was enough to send her into Fort Knox mode. "Silly me, wanting to hear I'm someone's soul mate."

"Is that what you want from me?" he asked—rather than reassuring her.

"I want you to want it," she said, defeat already weighing her down. Knowing the path from here would be harder, more painful than what they'd tread before. She was not a replacement. Not a transferable part in a design.

And yes, he wanted to be there for the girls. But did he love *her*?

The fact that he'd referred to them as a package deal dealt a blow to her heart. It'd been run through by a broadsword. Confirming her fears that she, Mary and Anna were stand-ins for a life he would never recover.

Naomi couldn't make him understand how she felt. She couldn't make him want the *here*, the *now*, and not just another round at the back *then*.

"I want us to help each other thrive as a team." She choked on the words as she pushed them past what felt like lead in her throat. "And all I see is the ways I hold you back from being who you're meant to be."

His hands fell away from her and he stepped back. Lips thinned into a line, and his deep brown eyes full of anger and sparks. "And I see you're no different than when we first met. Too afraid to risk your heart." He grabbed his parka and snapped for his dog. Tessie obediently leaped to her feet, already moving with speed toward the staircase. "Don't bother trying to drag out this argument any longer. I'll save you the trouble."

Without another word, he left her. No arguing. No fighting for her. Not even attempting to say what she wanted—needed—to hear. He'd initially said he wanted closure. And they'd gotten it.

She'd just been hiding from the truth. That the only closure she wanted was a fresh start to be with the man she loved.

And judging by the set of Royce's rigid shoulders as he walked away, that was never going to happen.

Twelve

Naomi had never felt less like going to work than today.

Reading over notes before her meeting with Glenna and Royce, she struggled for focus. Thank goodness her father and Jeannie were able to watch the twins for her. They were even going out of their way to bring them to her this afternoon, so she could nurse the babies then take them to their wellness checkup at the pediatrician's office.

Words on the printouts blurred. Her heart was in tatters from just a week away from Royce. They hadn't spoken since he'd left, and even if he'd called, she wouldn't have known what to say. Of course, she hadn't called him, either. The grief of this breakup overshadowed their other, the depth of what she'd lost so much more tangible.

But one foot in front of the other… She had to be here today for this meeting about the pipeline financing. Her children were in good hands. She'd hired a day nanny, who was basically watching Jack and Jeannie fawn over the twins. Still, Naomi couldn't help but recall the synergy of working with Royce to have the girls here at the office…

Her chest tightened at just the thought of their time as an almost-family. She blinked back tears and strode into the boardroom.

Game face carefully in place, she adjusted her weight on her heeled boots, entering the room for her meeting with all the bravado she could muster.

Business had to be done. The matter pressed into her chest, wearing another ache into her heart.

As she made eye contact with Glenna, Naomi registered pain and fear in her gaze.

Cocking her head to the side, Naomi opened her mouth to express confusion as Broderick placed a hand on Glenna's back. Concern lined his face, too.

Something terrible had happened. That much she understood. She could practically taste the unease lingering in the air of the well-lit boardroom. Worry racked Naomi, that chest-tightening feeling an all too familiar response these days.

Glenna's eyes grew shuttered and her expression became determined. "An emergency came up with Shana," she said, her voice shaky. "They hadn't told anyone yet, but she was expecting. She miscarried last night."

Naomi pressed a hand to her mouth. "Oh, no, I'm so sorry to hear that."

Her mind wandered to Mary and Anna, to an impossible what-if. She sent up a silent prayer of thanks for the health of her baby girls, and a second prayer of comfort for the obviously grief-stricken couple.

"This isn't their first loss." Glenna's low voice was raspy, no doubt from recently shed tears. "They've stopped sharing any news right away."

Naomi nodded, setting her binder on the table as she slipped into the chair at the head. "That's totally understandable."

She'd felt the same in telling people about her pregnancy, although the news had gotten out in spite of her efforts to keep it to herself. She'd been so upset with Royce for blurting out the news when she'd fainted. He'd been concerned, though. He was a good man, which made walking away from him all the tougher.

Broderick opened his briefcase on the conference table. "Glenna and I dug deeper into the numbers and we want to go over our thoughts with you before talking to Dad and Jeannie this afternoon. We noticed a trend in stock buy-ups and sell-offs that are affecting our bottom line."

"That's why we're short?" Naomi blinked fast, wondering how it could be that simple. And then, at the same moment, she remembered how Royce had been close to arriving at a similar conclusion. The numbers had been off. "Bad luck?"

Broderick shook his head, withdrawing a stack of bound printouts. "The timing is too suspicious for it to be coincidental. It would take a million-and-one odds for things to roll this way." He leaned back in the leather chair. "My gut—a very seasoned gut—tells me there's insider information being leaked. Someone who doesn't want this merger to happen."

Her stomach sank. "Who?" Naomi sat up straighter. All those fears about the merger. That the families couldn't trust one another. What if they'd made a grave mistake?

"The person I'm thinking about doesn't make sense." Broderick's eyes slid to his wife.

"Who?" Naomi pressed, needing answers. Whoever it was had not only sabotaged the merger, but had torpedoed Royce's research, his life's work.

And in spite of everything, that sent a surge of defensiveness through her for him. He didn't deserve this.

Broderick drummed his fingers on the stack of papers. "Glenna's new personal assistant. Milla Jones."

Milla?

That was the last person Naomi would have expected. Sure, she'd had the occasional sense that something was "off" when the woman was around. But insider trading?

Naomi was grateful that Broderick didn't suspect

anyone in the family. "She's new to the company. Very low level." She turned to Glenna. "What do you think?"

Her sister-in-law thumbed the corner of her copy of the printouts. "No company is safe from someone who is computer savvy."

Having a face to put with these problems was a step toward being able to fix them. If they could, that would mean Royce would be back at the company on a regular basis. Naomi should be glad for him. And she was. Only now… Their paths would cross regularly. How would she handle that without losing her mind—and her heart?

She swallowed down the lump of emotion in her throat and focused on what she had to do, or what was right—making Royce's innovations a part of the company. "What do you think is the best approach?"

"I say we ask her to take a lie detector test," Glenna said. "We're within our rights to do that, aren't we, Naomi?"

"With the contract she signed, we could…" She visualized the document, certain of the legal precedent, but wanting more information first.

Broderick leaned forward, hands pressing on the oak table. "That would also risk tipping off whoever she's working for."

Royce's career was riding on this. Naomi had drawn him into the company, and even if he didn't love her, she could still give him this one thing—his work. His dream.

"Quite frankly," she said, "I don't think we have time to set a trap. We need to plug this leak now if we want there to be any chance of incorporating Royce Miller's work into the next phase of our construction."

"No use waiting. Let's get this settled." Glenna clapped her hands together. "Perhaps you should handle the questions, use those lawyerly skills of yours."

Nodding, Naomi tapped the pager, ready for the battle, a fight she would relish tackling.

"Ms. Jones, please come in." While waiting, she glanced out the window at the stunning Alaska mountain range They had to succeed in getting Royce's designs online. The beauty of this wild land counted on research like his to thrive.

With a deep breath, Naomi focused on the task at hand, sitting straighter in her ruffled work dress as the door swung open.

"Yes? What can I do for you?" Milla asked.

"You can sit and have a chat with us," Glenna said, gesturing to a chair at the boardroom table.

Glenna's assistant raised her brows, surprise coloring her features. And then there it was. The strangeness Naomi couldn't articulate. The way the young woman held their gazes felt…well, that was what she couldn't name.

Smoothing her blue, A-line dress, Milla sat.

Naomi fixed her with a pointed stare. "What

brought you to Alaska Oil Barons, Inc. to work? You're far away from home."

"I read about the position on an online job board." Milla moved her hands from the table to knot in her lap. "It sounded like an adventure."

"We've had an incident," Naomi said, watching for a reaction in the woman's eyes—which quickly became guarded, blank almost. More telling than an overt twitch.

Milla Jones was hiding something.

Even if they didn't plan to use a lie detector test at this juncture, it would be interesting to see how the woman reacted to the possibility. "We've discussed having you take a polygraph."

"No need," Milla said.

Broderick leaned forward, elbows on the table. "You're refusing?"

"Not at all." Milla crossed her arms over her chest. "I'm offering to tell you what you want to know now."

Naomi regarded her warily. "And what would that be?"

Flattening her palms on the conference table, Milla stated baldly, "I know who's responsible for your stock flow problem."

Glenna gasped. Broderick's eyes narrowed.

Naomi held herself immobile, surprised but wary. She hadn't expected the woman to offer up information so easily. "So you're admitting to being a party to insider trading?"

"I'm giving you what you want, since you've already figured out the worst parts yourself." Milla's face became set in hard, bitter lines. With her voice defiant, she looked and sounded nothing like the smooth, accommodating professional of the past weeks. She was a damn good actress.

Naomi didn't appreciate the woman's flippancy—at all. Time for Milla to feel the weight of what she'd done. "Pardon me if I don't find this a joking matter, and perhaps you shouldn't, either. You're admitting to committing corporate espionage."

"I have information. You need it. And trust me—" she smiled darkly "—you'll never think of the right questions to ask on your own."

Broderick swept the air with both hands. "Then by all means, say your piece."

Milla's gaze flicked to each of them before she spoke. "You're a family of power. Power doesn't always treat others fairly."

"You'll have to do better than that," Broderick barked, launching a stare-down.

Finally, Milla looked away. "I don't know who the mole is. But I do know who, um, *he* or *she* reports to."

"Who would that be?"

"The same people responsible for the plane crash that killed your mother, Mary Steele." The words felt like bombs shaking Naomi's foundation.

Shock knocked the air out of Naomi's lungs over the unexpected words, bringing a fresh wash of pain.

Reeling from the information, she reached for her brother's hand and squeezed tightly for comfort, until her fingers numbed.

A desperate need for the truth clawed at her. "And our sister Breanna."

"Are you absolutely certain she died?"

Naomi couldn't have heard what she thought she had. No way would this woman be so cruel. How dare she? There had been proof. But before she could rip into the woman for her heartless gall, a gasp sounded from behind her, one that hitched with a groan of pain.

She turned to see her father in the doorway, holding Anna, while Jeannie stood behind him, cradling the other twin.

Naomi wanted to go to her dad and comfort him, but she couldn't move, stunned still, processing all this through a haze of shock. That someone could toss out such a false hope tore her apart.

Jack Steele's face was twisted with grief, pain, then anger. Glenna leaped to her feet and took both infants in her arms, leaving quickly. Jeannie stepped up to place a comforting—or restraining?—hand on Jack's arm.

Whoever this Milla Jones woman was, she was sick. Twisted. Naomi wanted to scream until her throat was raw. To throw things until she battered holes in the wall. Anything to get out the pain that woman had brought on by suggesting Breanna might not have died. Her family had worked so damn hard for closure.

She had grieved so hard in search of closure.

Having that ripped away with a simple sentence was beyond imaginable.

Because there was no way Breanna could be alive. There had been DNA tests run on remains.

Hadn't there?

Her sister was dead. It was cruel of this woman to dangle the hope that Breanna could be out there somewhere, to offer them a hope that couldn't be, a hope that would deny them closure forever.

Naomi's hands shook. More than air, she wished she had Royce at her side, the way her father had Jeannie.

But no matter how much it hurt, Naomi was done leaning on Royce's strong shoulders. It wasn't fair to him, to either of them, when he would never love her.

Royce couldn't remember when he'd last needed time in the saddle like this.

The past week without Naomi had been hell.

So he did what he did best. He pulled away.

He sequestered himself and tacked up, taking solace in the ritual of tightening the girth, slipping the bit into the bay horse's mouth.

In the freedom afforded by the open trail, the tufts of falling snow.

Sinking into the saddle, he took off on horseback, in a gallop that allowed him to examine these last few weeks.

Heading up the mountainside, he held the reins loosely. Remembered how sensitive this gelding was to the slightest touch. He needed to be gentle and open, give the horse his head. When he'd heard about Milla Jones's stunt from Broderick, Royce had wanted to run to Naomi's side, to be there for her.

Even if the woman's claims were false, she'd stirred a wealth of turmoil in both families, resurrecting grief. But strangely, she'd also unified their bonds, since they were all working together now. Chuck's wife, Shana, had notified private eye connections to investigate the issue. Milla had taken off and no one could find her.

Turning a corner in the trail, Royce guided the bay on up the mountainside, slowing to a trot as he navigated the thicker parts of the forest, finding more clarity the higher they went. Feeling alive and connected.

The way the Steeles and Mikkelsons came together in spite of something that should have sent them all into a tailspin…it blew him away. And yes, it surprised him, too.

So often, he'd viewed the two large families as a distraction from his work. From Naomi. But seeing the way they leveled one another out now, the way they functioned as a unit despite their differences, gave him a balanced perspective. For the first time,

Royce realized that he wished he could have been a part of the effort.

The balance.

It was a scientific principle. A law of the universe. And one Royce couldn't seem to master in his personal life.

He slowed the gelding to a walk, keeping his weight centered, a light hand on the saddle horn. The bay shook his black mane with a snort.

As he looked at the deserted woods all around him, Royce realized it was damn difficult to help when he was living in solitude. Naomi and her family were there for each other, and yes, sometimes that came with crowds and static. But it also came with a wealth of support. Of common resolve. Dynamic energy.

He'd always been a man of science. How had he missed seeing the balance that he and Naomi could bring to each other's lives?

Her big family showed him a world of extended strength. And yes, maybe he'd been holding back from commitment because all this was too much to lose.

Naomi was too special to lose. She wasn't a substitution or replacement for anyone. She was a once-in-a-lifetime love.

But then hadn't he lost her already by walking away?

He loved her.

He had never stopped, really. He'd only deluded himself.

She was a part of him and there was no escaping that. If he could only convince her how he felt.

And he didn't intend to wait another day to tell her.

He hadn't planned on going to the gala celebrating Jack and Jeannie. But he realized now that he had to be there for Naomi. A swift, light tug to the right and the bay turned around. Responsive. As if he, too, could feel the building need. The urgency swelling in Royce's heart.

Light pressure from his calves sent the horse into a working trot as they wound through the trees. Then they were at the edge of the woods, with open land in front of them. Open for all his possibilities. More pressure to the horse's sides sent the bay into a headlong gallop.

The racing horse matched his racing realization. There was nowhere else Royce would rather be than by Naomi's side.

For the rest of his life.

Naomi adjusted the black velvet cape over her red satin gown, scrambling to gather up her ragged nerves and courage before stepping out of the limo and into the masquerade-themed gala.

Into the chaos.

It'd been a helluva week.

Shana was recovering, Chuck by her side. Milla

had been fired, and so far the investigator hadn't found anything out of the ordinary about her or her family in Canada, where she'd returned. Having her out of reach worried Naomi. What if she tipped off someone else? Bottom line, they didn't have enough cause to call the cops, but Milla had left a boatload of questions behind.

And Naomi wrestled with a niggling twinge that maybe, just maybe, there was truth to her insinuation that Breanna was alive.

Cutting the thought short, she popped open a compact, investigating the subtle smoky eye makeup Delaney had promised would make her feel fierce. But the mirror only served to remind Naomi of her nightmare.

She had been dreaming about Breanna, envisioning what she would look like. Seeing her in a mirror, unable to tell if it was her own face or her sister's reflected back.

Snapping her compact shut, Naomi closed down the thoughts that would have her crying her smoky eyes into a mess. She took a moment to center herself before stepping out into the cool winter air, tugging her velvet cape tighter to shield her back-baring dress from the elements. Her jeweled velvet shoes were safe from the snow on the red carpet arranged by the event organizers.

Placing one high heel in front of the other, she took in the sight. Twinkling string lights led up to the Steele office building. Snow gathered on the ground bathed the whole scene in an idyllic winter wonderland.

In her peripheral vision, Naomi saw a familiar silhouette.

Her heart hammered and her chest convulsed as the tall, dark man approached, impeccably turned out in a sleek black tuxedo.

Royce.

Had she been holding her breath for long? She certainly felt light-headed.

He fell into step with her as she traversed the red carpet, passing the smaller trees adorned with twinkling white lights. The way the lights were arranged made them appear like up-close constellations. Perfect for wishing.

Which she did as she passed by. Needing her night to go well. Wishing for some sort of stability as her whole world felt uprooted.

The doorman smiled, opening the Steele office to her and Royce.

Ruggedly handsome as ever, Royce picked up two masks from the table full of beaded and feathered creations. "You look absolutely beautiful."

"Thank you… Why are you here?" Her voice came out whispery as she took the mask he handed her, an ornate Venetian recreation adorned with golden accents and decadent feathers. She fastened it to her face, looking at him.

"I'm here for you."

"That simple?"

"Let's just say I've reacquainted myself with the universal laws of balance and realized I need to be with my equal and opposite tonight. Unless you have another date." His burgundy-and-gold mask somehow intensified the amber flecks in his brown eyes.

"You know I don't." She swallowed, thankful that her mask obscured her cheeks.

"Good. Then we won't be late, since I won't have to remove the guy." He offered her his arm.

A whisper of apprehension spiraled through her. She knew now how much it hurt to get close to him when he couldn't open his heart to her, but something prodded her to take what he offered this evening, this one last time.

The live jazz band was already playing in full force, a trumpet cutting into the greeting area. A beacon. A call to dance and to mingle.

How hard it was to focus on the party with her heart pounding from Royce's nearness. The old pull of desire was as sharp as ever. Sharper, even, since she knew she couldn't heed that wild call to lose herself in his touch.

They moved on in beneath the gold and white tulle that hugged the ceiling. Guests in masks filtered through, posing for pictures with each other in front of the Renaissance-inspired art installation that tied the masquerade's theme together.

Glimmering gowns pressed to dark tuxedos kept catching her eye, making her aware of the way romance seemed to hang in the air. But more than romance, she realized. People embraced each other. Steele and Mikkelson families hugged and toasted.

Tonight, there were no sides, no enemies.

Just love. In all its forms.

Jack and Jeannie greeted the guests as they arrived, so many people in their circle of family and close friends. Only the immediate family knew about what Milla Jones had claimed, and looking at Jack, no one would have guessed. However, Naomi saw the way Jeannie carried more of the conversation for him. She stroked his wrist lightly, which looked like simple affection, but to the finer tuned eye was a comforting gesture.

Perhaps for the first time since her family was put on a collision course with the Mikkelson clan, Naomi saw her father and Jeannie. Really saw them and noticed the way they continuously offered each other support. She could see it as they stood together, unified.

They truly loved each other.

There *were* second chances at love.

It sounded so simplistic. And perhaps it could be. Royce hadn't bolted, no matter how many times she pushed him away. He stayed if not by her side, at least close enough to reach. Seeing him here tonight blew her away as he powered on, even though not at all in his favorite venue, but still checking the boxes.

And looking damn fine in the process.

He'd found balance. She was the one tipping the scales too far in one direction.

Had she been wrong to push him away again?

A crescendo swelled from the stage, signaling the end of the song, followed by a drumroll. A spotlight shot down to the side stage.

Revealing Royce?

"I'm honored to join in the festivities celebrating Jack and Jeannie's marriage. They are an inspiration in both their personal and business worlds." Royce lifted his champagne glass, the cut crystal refracting the spotlight, sending prisms through the room like northern lights, bathing everyone in fire. "I know they've requested no gifts, but I have an offer I feel certain they won't be able to refuse, and I challenge others here to join in. I'm contributing personally to their oil pipeline safety initiative. All profits from my patent on the new equipment will go directly toward seeing the project come to life."

In the crowd, Birch Montoya lifted his glass, as well. "Count me in for an extra million."

Gasps went through the packed room, before a round of applause swelled and other voices shouted their intent to join in. As it faded, Royce lifted his glass again. "To Jack and Jeannie. To Alaska Oil Barons, Inc."

Naomi soaked in the vision of Royce onstage, unable to deny the rush of excitement that he wouldn't be fading away. He'd done this for her and her family. And he'd done it in such a public way. He'd embraced this crowd. Stood strong in the harsh spotlight with a new ease. For her.

The applause faded and he made his way toward her, grinning.

"I don't know what to say. Thank you doesn't come close to being enough." Her hands shook so, she had to place her champagne flute on a passing waiter's tray. "You're still going to work with the company, aren't you?"

"Of course," he said. "Let's step aside and talk. Or rather, I have something I need to say."

Her stomach did a flip—half hope and half fear of hoping.

His callused fingertips grazed her hand, their palms joining together as he wound through the crowd. Champagne glasses clinked as they passed by. But he never let her go.

After pushing down on a brass door handle, he brought her out on a balcony where heat lamps had been placed to chase away the winter chill.

Dropping her hand, he led her to the edge to view the bay. "The party came together well. A solid launch of the two families merging."

"It seems surreal, given all the turmoil with the possibility that Breanna..." Naomi's throat closed and she couldn't continue.

He pulled her to his chest, her mask crinkling. She drew in the comfort and spark of being close to him. She'd missed him. She needed him. She closed her eyes and breathed in the familiar scent of his aftershave.

But why was he here?

She licked her lips, swallowing to moisten her dry mouth. "But there's nothing I can do about that tonight." She angled back. "This is an evening for celebration. For Dad and Jeannie."

"For us, too, I'm hoping."

Her heart leaped to her throat and she bit her lip to keep from blurting out right here and now how much she loved him. She needed to listen, hear him out.

He gestured toward the bay just as fireworks lit up the sky. The blue light was reflected in the water. Another firework erupted. And another. A vibrant display shimmered through the night dome.

"Oh, how gorgeous. Dad must have ordered them from the event planners. I wish I had thought of it..."

Royce took her hand in his again. "I arranged it. Timed it even."

Surprise stunned her into silence for a moment, and she lifted her mask to see him more clearly. He hadn't put his on again after his moment in the spotlight inside.

"That was thoughtful of you to do for them," she observed carefully, telling herself not to read too much into the gesture.

"They're for you," he said. "As I said, timed. For right now."

The romance of that twined around her heart. Her breath hitched in her throat, hope gaining ground fast. "They're stunning."

"*You* are stunning."

She smoothed a hand down the lapel of his custom tailored tux. "You clean up quite nice yourself. Although I do have a partiality to your MIT sweat-shirt." She looked up at him. "Your announcement about the donation was...astounding. I'm almost afraid to hope..."

"It's okay to hope." He traced her jaw with his thumb, his touch unleashing feelings she'd been trying madly to hold back.

"That seems rather intangible coming from a scientist."

"The more I learn, the more I realize there are things in life that defy logic. You, us, what we have together—one of a kind—is worth fighting for."

One of a kind. Not a replacement. But their own unique, beautiful bond.

From the light in his eyes, she could see he, too, was hopeful.

"One of a kind." Naomi added, "I agree." Ready. She was so very ready to have him in her life. No more reservations.

A smile spread across his face as he hooked an arm around her shoulders. "You must know I love you. Even when I tried to tell myself otherwise, I couldn't stop."

"I do understand. It's scary, but so very exciting. I love you, too, Royce Miller."

"Thank God," he said, with a sigh of relief before he pulled her into his arms and sealed her words with a kiss that sizzled even more than those fireworks.

They had loved each other even before that first breakup. They just hadn't learned how hard they had to work to make that love last. To protect it. Cherish it. Put it first. The connection was deeper now. Stronger. Unbreakable.

He might not have used the words *soul mate* when she wanted, but he was constantly showing her with the things he did. He wasn't just there for the twins, he was there for her, too, making sure she had everything she needed, somehow knowing that if the babies were safe and happy, she would feel safe and happy, as well. Yes, he loved the girls, but he loved her, too. Just as she loved him.

Royce rested his forehead against hers. "Naomi, you are my love, my life, and yes, my soul mate."

She could hear the emotion in his words, felt the truth in the hitch in his voice. She'd known he loved her daughters, and that meant the world to her for them. But now she knew he also wanted—and was in love with—her, as deeply as she wanted and loved him.

Smiling, she angled back. "I think we have some celebrating of our own to do."

He grinned at her. "Lead the way."

"How about side by side?" She looped her arms around his neck. "Right after you kiss me again."

"Yes, ma'am," he said, with a smile and a promise.

A promise he fulfilled.

Epilogue

One Month Later

Some women dreamed of getting married in a church, husband holding her hands.

Some visualized saying their vows at home, man of her dreams gazing adoringly into her eyes.

But Naomi couldn't think of anywhere better to begin her wedded life than on a glacier. Officially marrying her forever love, the father of her twins.

Now, standing in the receiving line to greet their family, who'd flown in on seaplanes, Naomi was dancing on air with how their ceremony had been everything she'd hoped for and more. Her in a long-sleeved wedding gown and formfitting white satin jacket with white fur around the hood. Him in a tuxedo and Texas cowboy hat and boots.

Violins and a small harp had played modernized versions of old Inuit tunes, the songs her grandmother had loved best. A way to honor someone special to her, and feel like her grandmother's spirit was there, smiling down on them. Naomi stood beneath a large Inuit tapestry serving as a canopy for the reception food table, the simple decor just right for their remote glacier venue.

And the backdrop for it all? Her magnificent Alaska homeland, mountains capped with snow. Stretches of crystal water dotted with other, smaller pieces of ice.

The world glittered, humming with life and joy, no other adornment needed. The Alaskan outdoors was a place where Naomi and Royce had always been in harmony, a place they both hoped to spend more time together. The hubbub of her loved ones around her, the hum of family, were a welcome part of her life.

She and Royce had spent the past month making plans for this celebration and how to blend their lives. She was ready to branch out of the Steele compound and claim some dedicated space for their family. They'd kept the glass igloo retreat for camping vacations with the twins, but realized they needed more room, not just the occasional getaway cabin. A larger place to accommodate their own family that would also give Royce the square footage needed for cave time. They'd bought a sprawling home on the outskirts of Anchorage, complete with a barn that sported a loft office being custom renovated for Royce.

And they'd definitely need the extra space once Anna and Mary would be crawling to get the brightly colored abacuses Royce had bought them.

Shana and Chuck stopped in front of them now, shoulder to shoulder without touching, their relationship seeming as strained as always. Shana had been digging deep into Milla Jones's past and following leads about the woman's disappearance into the Canadian landscape. Naomi felt confident that if there were answers to be found, Shana would unearth them.

Clutching Naomi's hands, Shana leaned in to whisper, "Don't you worry, if your sister is out there, we will find her."

Naomi squeezed her fingers. "I know you will. Thank you." She hugged her hard, then said, "Thank you, too, for watching Anna while we're away."

"My joy," Shana said, a hint of yearning in her eyes that spoke of longing for a baby of her own. "It's worked out well that Delaney and Birch can take Mary."

Naomi's eyes went to her sister, who swayed from side to side holding the baby, Birch staring over her shoulder. Just beyond them, Jack and Jeannie shared a private moment at the side of the gathering. Jeannie twirled under Jack's arm for a kiss.

Royce chuckled. "Hopefully, both girls will get some sleep when they're not waking each other up all night to play."

Naomi rolled her eyes, laughing along with him. "Um, more like you waking them up to rock them."

She loved how he adored her daughters as his own. How could she have ever worried? Royce's heart was big enough to love them all.

They were going to spend their honeymoon at the igloo cabin where they'd met, hiking and exploring, for a couple days before the twins would join them at their large new home on the water, the main renovations complete. Their latest remodeling idea included a sauna with a glass roof, perfect for romantic moments spent watching the northern lights. Now that they'd unlocked the secret to balance in their lives, she'd taken so much joy from finding ways to nurture their needs as a couple, and as strong-willed individuals, too.

She hooked her arm in his, leaning in to whisper, "It's everything I ever dreamed of."

"Me, too," he answered, his eyes full of love and commitment as he bent to kiss her.

They'd worked hard for their happily ever after, but were the stronger for it. Their bond now was solid. Unbreakable. She would count on Royce forever, and she couldn't wait to be the woman he turned to day after day for the rest of their lives.

The feel of his lips on hers stoked the fire in her

veins for him. Her husband. Every kiss even more exciting than the last.

She angled back, his eyes warm on hers with an answering fire as the music from the quartet crescendoed. "Can I have this dance?"

He tipped his Stetson with a roguish glint in his gaze. "This one and every one thereafter. Consider your dance card full, my love."

* * * * *

Passion and turmoil abound in the lives
of the Alaskan Oil Barons!
Nothing is as it seems.
Will they find Milla Jones? Will Chuck and Shana
heal their fractured marriage?
Is Breanna alive?
Find out the answers and so much more when the
Steeles and Mikkelsons return in four more
thrilling books, available November and
December 2017,
and January and February 2018!

And don't miss a single twist in the
first four books of the
ALASKAN OIL BARONS
from
USA TODAY *bestselling author Catherine Mann:*

THE BABY CLAIM
THE DOUBLE DEAL
THE LOVE CHILD
THE TWIN BIRTHRIGHT

COMING NEXT MONTH FROM

Available June 5, 2018

#2593 BILLIONAIRE'S BARGAIN

Billionaires and Babies • by Maureen Child

When billionaire Adam Quinn becomes a baby's guardian overnight, he needs help. And his former sister-in-law is the perfect woman to provide it. She's kind, loving and she knows kids. The only complication is the intense attraction he's always tried to deny...

#2594 THE NANNY PROPOSAL

Texas Cattleman's Club: The Impostor • by Joss Wood

Kasey has been Aaron's virtual assistant for eight months—all business and none of the pleasure they once shared. But the salary he offers her to move in and play temporary nanny to his niece is too good to pass up—as long as she can resist temptation....

#2595 HIS HEIR, HER SECRET

Highland Heroes • by Janice Maynard

When a fling with sexy Scotsman Brody Stewart leaves Cate Everett pregnant, he's willing to marry her...*only* for the baby's sake. No messy emotional ties required. But when Cate makes it clear she wants his heart or nothing, this CEO better be prepared to risk it all...

2596 ONE UNFORGETTABLE WEEKEND

Millionaires of Manhattan • by Andrea Laurence

When an accident renders heiress Violet an amnesiac, she forgets about her hookup with Aidan...and almost marries the wrong man! But when the bar owner unexpectedly walks back into her life, she remembers everything—including that he's the father of her child!

#2597 REUNION WITH BENEFITS

The Jameson Heirs • by HelenKay Dimon

A year ago, lies and secrets separated tycoon Spence Jameson from analyst Abby Rowe. Now, thrown together again at work, they can barely keep it civil. Until one night at a party leaves her pregnant and forces Spence to uncover the truths they've both been hiding...

#2598 TANGLED VOWS

Marriage at First Sight • by Yvonne Lindsay

To save her company, Yasmin Carter agrees to an arranged marriage to an unseen groom. The last things she expects is to find her business rival at the altar! But when they discover their personal lives were intertwined long before this, will their unconventional marriage survive?

YOU CAN FIND MORE INFORMATION ON UPCOMING HARLEQUIN® TITLES, FREE EXCERPTS AND MORE AT WWW.HARLEQUIN.COM.

HDCNM0518

SPECIAL EXCERPT FROM

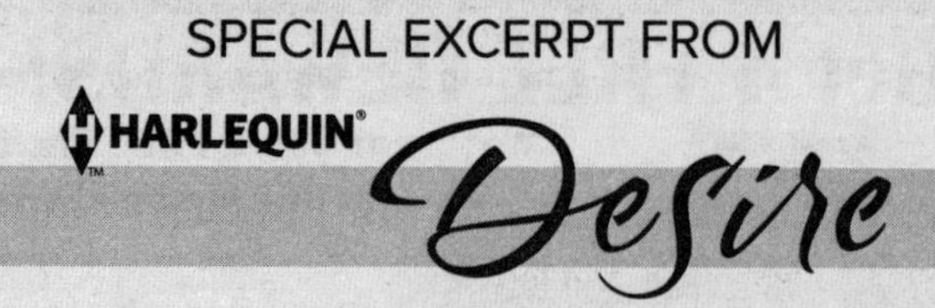

A year ago, lies and secrets separated tycoon Spence Jameson from analyst Abby Rowe. Now, thrown together again at work, they can barely keep it civil. Until one night at a party leaves her pregnant and forces Spence to uncover the truths they've both been hiding...

Read on for a sneak peek at REUNION WITH BENEFITS by HelenKay Dimon, part of her ***JAMESON HEIRS*** *series!*

Spencer Jameson wasn't accustomed to being ignored.

He'd been back in Washington, DC, for three weeks. The plan was to buzz into town for just enough time to help out his oldest brother, Derrick, and then leave again.

That was what Spence did. He moved on. Too many days back in the office meant he might run into his father. But dear old Dad was not the problem this trip. No, Spence had a different target in mind today.

Abigail Rowe, the woman currently pretending he didn't exist.

He followed the sound of voices, careful not to give away his presence.

A woman stood there—*the* woman. She wore a sleek navy suit with a skirt that stopped just above the knee. She embodied the perfect mix of professionalism and sexiness. The flash of bare long legs brought back memories. He could see her only from behind right now but that angle looked really good to him.

Just as he remembered.

Her brown hair reached past her shoulders and ended in a gentle curl. Where it used to be darker, it now had light brown highlights. Strands shifted over her shoulder as she bent down to show the man standing next to her—almost on top of her—something in a file.

Not that the other man was paying attention to whatever she said. His gaze traveled over her. Spence couldn't exactly blame him, but nothing about that look was professional or appropriate. The lack of respect was not okay. As far as Spence was concerned, the other man was begging for a punch in the face.

As if he sensed his behavior was under a microscope, the man glanced up and turned. His eyebrows rose and he hesitated for a second before hitting Spence with a big flashy smile. "Good afternoon."

At the intrusion, Abby spun around. Her expression switched from surprised to flat-mouthed anger in the span of two seconds. "Spencer."

It was not exactly a loving welcome, but for a second he couldn't breathe. The air stammered in his lungs. Seeing her now hit him like a body blow. He had to fight off the urge to rub a hand over his stomach. Now, months later, the attraction still lingered…which ticked him off.

Her ultimate betrayal hadn't killed his interest in her, no matter how much he wanted it to.

If she was happy to see him, she sure hid it well. Frustration pounded off her and filled the room. She clearly wanted to be in control of the conversation and them seeing each other again. Unfortunately for her, so did he. And that started now.

HDEXP0518